BONDAGE

THE GREAT EPIC - I

BONDAGE

THE STORY OF BHISHMA

NARENDRA KOHLI

Nine BOOKS

4695, 21-A, Daryaganj, New Delhi 110 002
Nine Books is an imprint of Vani Prakashan

Branch

Ashok Rajpath, Patna 800 004

Phone : +91 11 23273167 Fax : +91 11 23275710

www.vaniprakashan.in
vaniprakashan@gmail.com
sales@vaniprakashan.in

THE GREAT EPIC-1
BONDAGE : THE STORY OF BHISHMA
by Narendra Kohli
Translated by Mozez Michael
Translation sponsored by Vani Prakashan

ISBN : 978-93-5229-489-3
Novel

First Edition

Price : ₹ 395

Printed at Yash Printographics, Noida-201 301 (Uttar Pradesh)

1

It was impossible.

It was hard to imagine that such an event could occur. Even after it had occurred Devavrata found it hard to believe. How could this have happened?

Impossible, impossible, Devavrata kept on repeating to himself in his mind.

But King Shantanu's chariot had passed by - That was the truth.

Even as a large crowd of nobles and general public thronged Vardhman, the gateway to Hastinapur, embellished exclusively to greet King Shantanu, he did not, so much as even acknowledge their presence as his chariot sped past them, leaving them utterly dazed and flabbergasted.

Among them was Devavrata, who was King Shantanu's son, but he was as bewildered as the general public.

He had spent his early years without a parent; his merciless mother wanted him to be reared up by his father who was too distraught by his mother's departure to even acknowledge the child's existence.

Deserted by his wife, Shantanu abandoned his son to be brought up at various ashrams under the stringent observation of the patron sages.

Handed back to his father, Devavrata saw a flicker of parental love which proved too short-lived. He raised his hands to touch his father's feet only to drop them in dejection as his father's chariot whizzed passed him. Why should he, in the first place, harbour any expectation from his father, a father who hardly missed him?

His filial leanings, though, soon got over that murmur.

Presently his thoughts were concentrated on his father, whose recent demeanour betrayed indisposition. Maybe the separation from his wife was behind that. Devavrata would often contemplate on the significance and power of love, affection, happiness, sorrow, expectations and disappointment. Anyway, he was determined to detect the cause and find the remedy.

Thus he rode his chariot to meet his father. He was not to be deterred by any criticism, any unsavoury remarks.

2

The royal palace wore an unusually deserted look. An eerie calm prevailed in the immediate surroundings. The welcoming mirth and hustle-bustle that greets a king back to his kingdom from a journey was conspicuously missing.

Devavrata virtually forced himself into his father's chamber and found him in deep melancholy and pain. It took the king quite a while to notice his son's presence. If the king was unwell, why was the official physician not informed? Devavrata asked his father who brushed aside the question as futile.

"There is no use," Shantanu said.

"Why?"

"Because I am not sick. I am distressed. No physician can cure me of my worries."

Shantanu's discourse revealed that he still regretted and mulled the loss of his other seven sons who were offered to the river Ganga by their mother. "Why should Ganga take away my seven sons?" he groaned.

"Now you are my only son," Shantanu returned to Devavrata, "and I have always felt that the father of an only son is far more miserable than one who has no son."

As Devavrata wondered what his father meant by that, Shantanu carried on.

"You are a warrior, my son," he said, "always ready to fight. But even the most accomplished warrior must meet his end one day. What if you are killed in a battle, what will happen to me, to the Hastinapur empire, to our lineage? How will I attain salvation?"

Devavrata was alarmed. Did his father have his son's marriage on his mind? Though his own parents' turbulent conjugal life had left him with little interest in assuming the fetters of a householder.

However, his fears were wiped out by what his father uttered next.

"I did not remarry after Ganga's departure. And I don't intend to even now. But one son ..." He resumed after a pause, "he who has no son has no fear of loss, but he who has but one son is always concerned about him."

"Worry not for me, sire. There is not one born yet on this earth who could martyr me."

"May your words be true, my son! But that's too little to assuage a father's agitated mind. Whenever I am reminded of the perishability of man's body, I think of my only son's untimely demise and my heart is filled with pain. Perhaps, you cannot imagine the agony of a father who has only one son."

Devavrata tried to convince his father, King Shantanu, that it was just a hang-over of a hectic hunting trip. But he knew his father was not satisfied. His gaze seemed to say: "Why don't you understand what I mean to say, Devavrata?"

3

Back in his palace, Devavrata was still haunted by his father's discourse. Was his father really afraid for his only son, that he would be killed in a war some day? But that could happen to even two sons, even a hundred. What number of sons would ensure the continuity of one's lineage?

Devavrata laughed at the thought. Why should a man ever crave the continuance of his clan? What is a man's life? Why should he want to live? Why that fear of death?

A son was essential to the Aryans as a warring race needs fighters. And, perhaps, therefore they linked a son to a man's emancipation. That possibly was the dogma of a warring society. A son was seen as an extension of a man's life. He was there to serve his father in his old age. Would a man be so concerned about his clan's survival if he were ensured care in his advanced age from his clan or community, Devavrata wondered. Why, his own mother had offered her seven sons to the Ganga and never bothered about any offspring? So with Devavrata. The recluses were not concerned with keeping their lineage alive; kings like Shantanu were. What did it imply? That Shantanu was a king and Devavrata a recluse?

But they belonged to the same clan, the same lineage. Was his father, then, considering his own marriage? Devavrata mused.

His father had been struck by kamdev arrow the

instant he saw Devavrata's mother beside the river Ganga. He was too enamoured of her to indulge in any enquiries about her. Obsessed with racial purity, an Aryan would normally dissect a woman's antecedents before entering into any alliance with her. His father, though, could not wait. He did not postpone the consummation of his desire for a moment and married her at once.

That attraction of the flesh could not sustain their household though. Living together and producing children was no household. To be bound in physical attraction and evade the desirable separation was but torture. The outward charm for Shantanu was nothing but a fowler's trap.

Whenever confronted with a comely female figure, Devavrata would get mortified. His conscience cautioned him. He could not free himself from such thoughts. Why could he not indulge in pleasure like his peers did? Was it because of his mother, who had offered her seven sons to the Ganga against her husband's will? And abandoned her husband when he prevented her from killing her eighth, namely Devavrata? In fact, she felt no attachment for her sons and no affinity for her husband. In spite of her long association with her husband, she had no regards for him.

Even Shantanu's father had not betrayed any trace of affection for him. Otherwise, as a parent, he should have cared for him.

No doubt parents produce children; but does that confer on them any right to dispose of their children as private assets? The incident showed them, particularly Shantanu's mother, in a bad light.

There was another perspective. His mother could have been a deity. She was, as some believed, goddess Ganga herself who, to remove the curse of the Vasus, had descended upon the earth and, against her will and nature, married an ordinary man and bore his children. Devavrata was not sure whether she was a human or a celestial being.

Contrary to popular claims, Devavrata felt that his father still yearned for her who never had any liking for him.

Abstention begets peace and equilibrium. But his father had plunged into disquiet after his mother's departure. Although Devavrata was the only one of his eight sons to survive, Shantanu never obliged him by his presence. He never saw him; never wished to see him. Devavrata dwelt at the ashrams (hermitages) of Vasistha and Parashurama; he stayed with Brihaspati and with Shukracharya. He knew not of his mother; his father ignored him-what would he do back in Hastinapur?

How had his father, who had left him in oblivion for all these years, suddenly become so concerned about his life and his own lineage? A volley of questions pestered him.

4

Devavrata approached the minister for an explanation and found his behaviour even more curious than his father's. The old man seemed to be comfortably ignorant of the king's plight.

When Devavrata broke the 'news' of the king's ill health, the old minister baffled him by disclosing that he was already aware of that. When asked why a treatment was not initiated, the minister hinted that it was a hopeless case and that only Devavrata could handle it.

"How?" asked the puzzled prince.

"The king suffers from a raging passion," proclaimed the minister.

So was it when he saw my mother and did not bother to enquire about her and conceded to all her terms, Devavrata mused and concluded that when his father was thus struck by carnal desires, the first casualty was his conscience.

Who was that woman who had thus rekindled the flame of passion in his father's bosom?

Further inquisition revealed that this time the king's emotions were stirred by a head boatman's extremely beautiful daughter. The king's proposal, though, was turned down by the boatman and, as the minister disclosed, the king had to return in lonely dejection. The head boatman's rider that the new queen's son should inherit the kingdom and the existing son lose all such rights had played the villain.

So it was all in Devavrata's hands at that juncture. He was confounded.

Did the minister want him to abdicate and forgo his rights? Was he representing his father? The king knew that his urge was unfair and, after therefore he had desisted from speaking to him, his own son. And that was why he desired another son, so that his unfair demand could somehow become feasible.

It was despicable on the king's part. Why, Devavrata hated him for that. How could a father be so blinded by the thrills of lust that he would thus lie to his son? Why couldn't he confess that his abstinence after his first marital separation was just forced. In fact, a man's bearings are determined by a woman's presence after. The world holds no charm for a man without a woman and the moment another woman appears he is captivated by her and the world's beauty is regained for him.

Though Devavrata did not fully endorse his father, who was now gripped by the head boatman's daughter demanding even his next generation's bondage, he was caught between contradictory urges. He was ready to part with his individual possessions, but his rights he would not forsake. He had to face the subject: posterity would accuse him of betraying his father, just for enjoying the pleasures of regality!

Devavrata found himself inadvertently filled with hostility against that unknown girl and her father. But that was not reasonable, he at once realised. There was nothing abnormal or unprecedented in the demands of the girl's father. The case of Kaikeyi's father demanding similarly from Dasaratha was but one example.

Who did he intend to please, Devavrata questioned himself. How could an old man's, in this case King Shantanu's, indiscreet attraction for a young girl provide any pleasure to anyone? What sensual pleasure would his father derive from this union? Pleasure is the sole product of love, selfless love that only gives and asks nothing in return. His father had not perceived that this kind of selfless love was missing from this matrimony. As for the girl, she was to collapse under the weight of her own complexes or subject others to misery through them. People would ridicule her and she would retaliate by punishing the weak, the weakest of them being King Shantanu. She would torture him and get tortured herself. Devavrata, therefore, decided to avert the imminent catastrophe for his father.

But another part of his mind condemned this as his selfish thinking. Devavrata was caught in a dilemma as he suspected that he aspired to acquire the pleasures of matrimony and kingdom for himself and not bestow them on his father.

5

Early one fine morning a host of armed cavaliers in festive dresses marched out of Hastinapur. The commander and the minister rode their respective chariots. Devavrata led from the front in his chariot. A vacant chariot with two maids was part of the small caravan while the usual wagons of provisions were absent.

The caravan halted on the outskirts of a boatmen's hamlet beside the river Yamuna. The city of Hastinapur was located on the banks of the Ganga, but the kingdom of Hastinapur was sandwiched between the two rivers. Most prominent Aryan cities were on either side of the Ganga, which formed their main lifeline. They were, though, not much associated with the Yamuna, which harboured celebrated cities like Mathura for chiefly safety reasons. However, various boatmen clans depended on the Yamuna for their livelihood. Rowing and fishing were the main businesses of the Kevata (boatmen) clans.

Guided by the minister, Devavrata walked forward and halted at the cottage of Dasaraja, the head boatsman, who greeted him ceremoniously.

Devavrata lost no time in coming to the point.

The head boatman, Dasaraja, was a wizened old man, though not sophisticated. His talks were, therefore, punctuated by such remarks as would have put off Devavrata under any normal circumstance. But the gravity of the situation and his mission kept him subdued.

Dasaraja was uninhibited and frank in his observations. "King Shantanu is in no way fit to be my daughter Satyavati's spouse," he said. "His only eligibility comes from his position as the king. And Satyavati would, if she ever did marry him, do so only with an eye upon eradicating her penury and attaining the kingdom of Hastinapur for her son whom she would not let inherit the fate of a boatman."

Devavrata did not flinch. He saw nothing ignoble in a man putting across his daughter's case in the most pragmatic manner he could manage.

The negotiations were concluded with Devavrata pledging to forsake any right to his kingdom in favour of Satyavati's eldest son.

"You know what it implies?" Dasaraja exclaimed.

"I do," Devavrata said. He was calm and smiling.

"You will cease to be the prince. You will not inherit your father's kingdom. Scaled down to an ordinary man, you will forfeit this great empire of the Kurus," Dasaraja spoke out in one breath.

"The is my vow, Dasaraja, and the Kurus' vow is in itself a testimony. Otherwise the king would have promised and taken away the girl. Devavrata would not be here then," Devavrata's submission was fraught with agitation.

"I beg you to calm down," the boatmen's chief implored. "I have not lived among the Kurus whose vow in itself is a testimony. I have ever lived among those whose vows are a mere sham and am not accustomed to accepting a promise as veracious ... Anyway," he resumed with a laboured smile, "you should not mind a weakened old man's doubts. Where there is parental affection, there are doubts, and where there are doubts, suspicion is also there."

Dasaraja was still not convinced. He wanted Devavrata to explain how he would deny his future sons their right to kingdom which they might lawfully demand. Suppose such a situation ever arose!

Devavrata was definitely caught off guard. He found himself being dragged into a labyrinthine state. It required some contemplation. Stirred back into sentience, Devavrata announced, "Dasaraja! I hereby solemnly pledge that my son, grandson, great grandson, no one will ever claim his royal inheritance from you, me, and your daughter. I do swear by the sun, the earth, and the air that I will remain a celibate all my life."

The minister was awfully shocked. "Gangeya! Prince!" he exclaimed, "What's this that you have done!"

Devavrata, however, betrayed no signs of sorrow, remorse, or conflict. He was rather happy over his triumph and liberation.

Dasaraja was all humility as he submitted, "O Prince! You are no mean man. You are a god. You are truly the sacred Ganga's son that flows through the earth so that she could irrigate her two banks and provide food, water and life to the hungry people dwelling thereon. You are truly great." His voice choked as he strained to finish, "And I am such an ignoble beast to have robbed you of all your weal, everything!"

Devavrata protested affectionately : instead of, "You know not, Dasaraja, what you have given out to me. Shun your emotions. Come, prepare for the departure of your daughter and my mother, the venerable Satyavati."

6

As Satyavati was escorted out of the unpretentious cottage by her mates, Devavrata was simply stunned by her gorgeous charm, which was all so incongruous in those surroundings. Was she a boatman's daughter, he wondered admiringly. Could she be a boatman's daughter? No, as Devavrata's host revealed, instead of : he had reared her, not begotten her.

She looked a notch above twenty five, an age when boatmen's daughters are usually married off. Maybe Dasaraja could not find a match for her. The boatman informed his royal visitor that "the boatmen who went out fishing found her floating in the Yamuna. She has the looks and glamour of a kshatriya (a warrior caste) king's daughter."

In the meanwhile, Satyavati had taken her friends' leave and rejoined her father. There were then a few emotional moments and gestures of a formal departure. The boatman was choked but distinct in his final words : instead of, "My daughter! I could not have detained you indefinitely here at my place. You were destined to be given out to a kshatriya king or prince. If not married willingly, they would have abducted you. I have obtained in this deal the maximum I could have for you. Now my prayer to God is that you may live happily at your husband's place."

Satyavati walked slowly to the chariot brought specially

for her and mounted it. Then Devavrata raised his arm to signal departure and the caravan took off.

Devavrata was deeply delighted and content to have Satyavati along. He felt quite light in his head and heart. He was elated to have fulfilled his father's wish at that crucial stage. His sacrifice was perhaps even greater than that of his ancestor Puru, who had forsaken his youth for a limited period to cure his father's senility. His sacrifice was greater in the sense that he retained his youth but renounced its pleasures, whereas Puru had gone old, both mentally and physically, following the barter, thus losing any interest in the urges of the body. Devavrata had relinquished all claims to kingdom. He had broken all shackles, all bonds. He had moved away from the lure of pleasure. He would bask in the blissful state of liberation.

Devavrata was also conscious of Satyavati's side of the story. Of course, she had gained queendom, but weren't her aspirations compromised? What was there to compensate it? She would never enjoy the company of those of her age, thoughts and conduct. Recalling the disparity between Dasaratha and Kaikeyi, "and Rama and Bharata", Ram and Bharata were not married to each other! Devavrata wondered how anyone could be happy in such marriages.

Was the story of a young woman marrying an old man going to be repeated in Kurus' palace as well? No, Devavrata convinced himself. There Kaikeyi wanted to exile Rama, but here he had exiled himself.

Devavrata thought about Satyavati and how she, who must have dreamed of a groom, a lover, a husband for herself, would relate to a lecherous old king lying on a golden bed in his royal chambers.

Devavrata's guilt raised his head. How could he assume that Satyavati's happiness lay in wealth? Only because she was a poor man's daughter? Why couldn't he see that by bringing Satyavati to the palace from the boatman's cottage he had actually deprived her of the comforts and pleasures available to her there? Most likely, the palatial wealth he anticipated for her would not translate into any happiness as such.

Yet, Devavrata solaced himself by the thought that before him Shravana Kumar and Rama, the son of Dasaratha, had endured their lot of suffering for their parents. His reasonings appeared as a thousand serpents entwined indistinguishably together, but for their so many heads.

Now it was a two-headed serpent confronting him about the validity of his decision to renounce physical pleasures. Was it aimed at escaping the physical woes or at securing his father's wishes? If the pleasures derived from wealth, power and woman were not substantial, he concluded, he had made no sacrifice: he had done only what was creditable.

So much about the father-son relationship. Devavrata's society recognised that the father had begotten and brought up the son and therefore the son was the sole property of his father. The son could never do enough for his father. Devavrata had passed many years in the proximity of nature. He knew a seed springs from the soil, becomes a tree, flourishes, withers, and returns to it-to be reborn. A father was just a medium. So why should he claim any rights?

A father was also a man, a bundle of human frailties. His intellect could also fail him. Why, then, only his desires, wishes, and judgements were acceptable? Devavrata was caught in a dilemma. There was no respite.

7

As the entourage marched forward, the imposing presence of her new 'son' Devavrata, brought to Satyavati's mind her other son, born of her liaison with the rishi (sage) Parashara.

She thought of her random encounter with the rishi. Her father the boatman, weighing all pros and cons, had assigned her the charitable task of ferrying the recluses who were supposed to be penniless and indifferent to the female beauty. Also, thus, there were to be no hassles involved for there was no transaction of money. It was, Dasaraja had concluded, safe for her growing up daughter.

Destiny though, had other plans for her. One fine day, rishi Parashara came to board her boat. Absorbed in himself, the rishi evinced no curiosity, no haste to know whether the boat would ever move and when.

When there were no passengers for quite a while, she decided to move with her lone occupant. The movement distracted the rishi's meditative mind. He looked at his ferrymaid and was enchanted by her pristine charm. His gaze met hers. He made no attempt to conceal his persistence. Satyavati was trembling; she felt nervous. She was clueless why that should happen to her, one who had been sailing the boat for quite some time and ferrying even young men across.

"You are so beautiful, Sunayana (one with large attractive eyes)!" The recluse spoke for once.

"My name is Satyavati," she retorted, wondering why he should call her 'Sunayana' without asking her name.

"You are very beautiful, Satyavati!" The recluse was informally specific now. "Your eyes, your lips, your neck, your figure, your carriage, O Satyavati! You know not how deeply you have shaken me."

Satyavati was fascinated. She had lost her composure. She had lost her way. She had strayed up to an obscure region, with an islet close by, where myriad lotus flowers bloomed.

The ensuing moments were irresistible. Satyavati was lured into what she would never otherwise do. She submitted herself, surrendered herself to the indomitable urge of her body.

First her father and then her mother got wind of what she had done or rather what was done to her. Their reactions were disparate. While the boatman had maintained a calculated calm, her mother was outraged.

Subsequent arrangements were made by her 'Baba', as she called her father. She was shifted from her village long before the actual event took place at the same islet. The child, a boy, was handed over by Satyavati to her recluse, the sage Parashara. "Take care of him," she said.

The sage took him in his arms with a sweet smile and said: "Worry not. You not being with me, he is all to me-Krishna Dvaipayana."

"Hope you won't despise him as an illegitimate child," Satyavati said without any scruples.

He smiled at her foolish remark. "Creation is a blessing, my lady!" he said. "Creation is the very goal of the creator. By contributing to it, we are only obeying the creator's commandment. We welcome the birth of every individual plant as the creator's smile, without ever bothering whether all morality was observed prior to its birth; whereas this is a human child."

Satyavati could but salute his sublimity, his

magnanimity. She returned.

Satyavati could never forget that she was denied the sage's companionship for he was not a prince. She had to part with little Krishna Dvaipayana for the king would not accept him, only a sage could. She had paid a very heavy price to be the king's bride. And when she had paid that price, she would claim and obtain her rights. She would materialise her Baba's dream.

Satyavati recalled King Shantanu's visit to her hamlet. It had created quite a ripple of curiosity in that rustic setting. The details were divulged by her Baba after the king had returned.

"We are fish-sellers, my daughter," the head boatman had said. "We try to sell our catch at the highest possible price. But ultimately it has to be sold at the price quoted by the buyer."

"I don't quite understand what you mean, Baba," Satyavati was puzzled.

"For me, you are very precious, my daughter. If it were within my powers, I would marry you off to a most handsome and strong kshatriya prince in the world. But they are beyond our reach. Luckily though, King Shantanu of Hastinapur is here to seek your hand in marriage. He is, however, much older than you. An old man compared to you."

Then, after a brief pause, he said: "Understand I intend to achieve the maximum out of this deal. I have told him that if he promises that your son will inherit the kingdom after him, I will marry you off to him."

Satyavati had nothing to say regarding the deal.

Then Baba told her about Devavrata, Shantanu's living young son and his doubt regarding him. What if he claimed his due? The doubt persisted even after Devavrata met him personally and took that oath.

Devavrata was a virtual riddle for the father-daughter duo. Baba's parting words at her departure were: "My daughter! I have laid the foundation and it is now upto you to erect a citadel over it. Have faith in yourself and none else. We know not what compelled Davavrata to make those sacrifices.... anyway, you will do well to stick to your rights, never letting them go."

Her chariot came to a halt and others followed suit. It was time for some rest and refreshment. She was seated beneath a dense leafy tree and served some exotic fruits and some water to drink.

Devavrata appeared personally and invited her most humbly to refresh herself.

The entourage finally reached the gateway of Hastinapur. She was rendered a ceremonious welcome there by the royal ladies. She was overawed by the magnificence of the palace which was going to be her home thereafter.

Devavrata greeted her at the palace gates and a group of very beautiful girls presented themselves to escort her into the royal abode. She followed them calm and quiet. Taking her cue from the majestic authority Devavrata enjoyed there, Satyavati decided that he could be her best help in that new environment.

8

Obviously, Shantanu had come to know of Devavrata's sacrifice. Even if reluctantly, Shantanu had braced himself to face his son for the first time after Satyavati's arrival. Suddenly, everything had changed between him and his son Devavrata. Anyway, he had been remotely informed of him-first his birth and then Ganga's attempt to drop him into the waters. Though he had saved his life, Shantanu never felt the need to know Devavrata just for that. To subdue his fury and aggressiveness born of Ganga's departure, Shantanu had taken to hunting that meant roaming in the forests for years. He thought he had, like Shiva, conquered Kama, the sexual desire. He remained away from his son and only learnt about him, his shifting abodes at various sages' ashramas, his exploits, his command over the scriptures, his sublimity... Then he had seen Satyavati beside the Yamuna and realised that he was not Shiva. The desire still occupied his mind.

Shantanu had then wished he had no son, so that he could marry Satyavati without any guilt. He realised that a son was not for comfort alone but could also be an obstacle. It would have been better if Ganga had offered the child to the Ganges and saved him the turbulence he was presently facing. He had recognised the force of sensual desire, how it numbed the senses beyond endurance. It had occurred to him that his own son, born of Ganga, had forced him beneath a cascade of fire, commanding him to 'burn.'

Now, the same Devavratasat before him, all so strong, so sacrificing.

"The vow you have taken," he managed to speak at last, "is not only difficult but impossible to fulfil. You have done a tremendous job. I can't give you anything. No one can ... the sort of man you are. I think you were not born to take anything;you will always give. You will be a giver to all the others, who will be beggars before you. I could not recognise you earlier. Now as I do, I give you a new name. For this vow of yours, you will henceforth be known as Bhishma."

"I have simply done my duty, Arya (noble one)!"

Shantanu looked intently at Devavrata. "Every father would wish to beget a son like you... rather, with a son like you, a father is worthy of taking pride in his own son, not capable of being proud of himself."

"O Noble one!"

"Yes, my son! It was my wish, not request."

"It did not merit request, sire. Being aware of his father's wish is enough for a son."

"Maybe, but a wish is something personal and becomes a social subject only when it culminates in action. An action is controlled by society, but a wish is not."

Shantanu continued: "Life offers certain moments of introspection, my son! My self-realisation has come not through my actions but through yours... The desire is bestial. But my conscience is aroused and recognises my moral limits. As iron filings are attracted furiously to a magnet, my blood had rushed towards Ganga and Satyavati. God has moulded me like that, my son. But, my conscience has always monitored me. I might have suffered pangs of torment, but I did not detain Ganga for my pleasure against her wish. I did not acquire Satyavati forcibly despite my kingly powers. Despite my kingly powers, I did not strip you of your due to get Satyavati......."

"Sire..." Devavrata tried to intercept but was promptly

checked.

"Listen, my son," Shantanu returned, "now since the barriers are broken, you would rather let me speak. I am exalted by your sacrifice this day. I am now a beggar before you, much belittled as a father. This moment is crucial and once it passes off, we will be left inhibited within our roles as father and son."

"Please, carry on!"

"Therefore do I submit that I am very mean when it comes to desire but my actions are never blemished. However, the fruits of your action have again fettered me into action. Passion acts as an intoxicant upon the conscience, my son! As long as passion prevails, conscience lies dormant. When the heat subsides, all appears as an idiot's hollow dream... Even as my conscience warns me even this day, I cannot contain the temptation of accepting the fruit of your action. The action is yours and the acceptance mine. Let us see to what extent the action will bind each of us."

"I have done this to rid myself of the bonds of action, sire!" Bhishma spoke low, "now I will neither marry nor will have a spouse or any children. I have blocked the path of action. Then any bonds?"

"Time is not ripe for that, my son! I can offer you nothing but blessings. Still, I wish to grant you a boon."

Bhishma looked up.

"I cannot rid you of the laws of Nature. But I bless you with a boon that would empower you to relinquish your vow on will. The bond is of your own making; I free you of any bonds from my side."

9

Goaded by his conscience, Shantanu hesitated at Satyavati's door. She was now his wife and he ought not to retrace his steps from her door. His conduct had to be in line with his status as a husband.

Shantanu entered Satyavati's chamber and was greeted formally with reverence. He patted her gently and requested her to sit down. She had to struggle to suppress the feeling of revulsion from manifesting itself. His sinister touch brought to her mind the thrilling memories of the recluse whose touch used to feel as a lotus petal on her body. But she dismissed the thought, purporting that if she wished to continue with her position as the queen consort and assume the role of queen mother in future, she must strive to please the king, even if despite herself.

Satyavati surveyed her body, which had so far been a means of pleasure for her and for the recluse as well! That pleasure was beyond social norms and position, beyond power, beyond money and beyond future. But, circumstances were changed now. Now, if she could satisfy the king's sexual urges, the kingdom of Hastinapur would be hers.

If Satyavati exhibited want of manners and etiquette, her environment and upbringing was to blame for that. Anyway, Shantanu had not chosen her for any such acquired attribute. He had fallen for her exceptional charm.

Their initial dialogue was fraught with half-explained

and half understood truths. Shantanu tried to be unambiguous. "The woman I desired as my first wife I did obtain, but she could not provide me any conjugal pleasures. Now my second choice is also conceded to me, but I may not provide her any conjugal pleasures."

"Why?" Satyavati was puzzled.

"It is the difference in our ages. Though I have that passion and I love you, I cannot ignore the fact that I am far too older than you. For your youth, I am an old man. I admit that I am not worthy of you. It is just my fascination for you. A married couple is much more than a man and a woman. There has to be much more between them. It was Bhishma who recognised my desire."

"Bhishma who?"

"Devavrata. I have given him this new name... for what he has done. No one else could have done that. It's not for me to judge whether his deed would be beneficial to me or not. For Nature has endowed every individual with some insane desire that would cause his destruction and the blame for that would also go to him."

Shantanu was into a candid introspection. The why and wherefore of his liking for Satyavati was her beauty and nothing else, which would last his life. He had liked her not as a human being but as an object. In fact, he had not procured her as a wife or to beget another son. At his age, like all men, he did not need a wife but a bed partner, whose beauty was the only requisite.

For a tired, exhausted and bored Satyavati, Shantanu's sermons were getting irksome. But Shantanu was her husband and disregarding him was not feasible. Again, the presence of this man brought to her mind the thought of that other man, her recluse, her tapasvi. How different she felt in the company of these two men!

Presently, Shantanu embraced Satyavati and was momentarily repulsed by her resistance.

Then, long after Shantanu had gone to sleep, Satyavati

drifted in a musing mode. She had thrown her lot with a stranger, a stranger who was a lot more prosperous, learned and perhaps even greater than her, a poor boatman's daughter. But her physical assets had positioned her at par with this man. Baba said that as the ocean loses its tranquility when faced with the full moon, so would King Shantanu be intimidated by Satyavati's charm and would run about as a trained dog at her hint. She had discovered the efficacy, the force of her power and now she had only to decide what was right for her, for its accomplishment would be within her capacity.

She mused over her memories of her tapasvi and also of their little son Krishna Dvaipayana. How she missed them! She would never endorse King Shantanu's view that Nature dismissed those of our desires which were not good for us. How could the denial of the recluse's presence in her life be good for her?

But there was another aspect to it. Suppose she had married the recluse, could he provide her all the comforts required for a tussle-free, smooth life? Won't she fight over the wants with her recluse and make life miserable for herself and others? Good that she followed her Baba's advice and made the present decision. Wasn't it Nature's discreet decision on her behalf? Nature had awarded her what she had desired. One must pay for what one got. Satyavati had acquired the comforts of life at the cost of her love.

And what about Devavrata Bhishma? Was it in her interest too to possess Bhishma as the son of this aged husband?

Baba had warned her to beware of Bhishma. "He could be your greatest enemy," Baba had professed.

Satyavati was perplexed.

10

"Who will instruct our children in arms and scriptures?" Satyavati's abnormally casual enquiry threw Shantanu off the guard for quite some moments. Who was she referring to? Why should Bhishma require any instructions in arms and scriptures at this stage and age? What did that pink on her face indicate?

"Are you expecting, Satya?" It was an afterthought drawing an immediate response from her. Yes, it was so.

"I was still immersed in the likelihood of a second child and here you talk of his instruction!"

"It is my first," retorted Satyavati and was instantly chastised by the memory of Krishna Dvaipayana, who was now being reared in that sage's cottage. But a vocal representation of that fact in the present circumstance would be disastrous, so the thought was at once dismissed.

Further conversation was rife with categorical remarks from Satyavati who was adamant on not sending her son to any ashrama run by a sage. She would prefer a competent home tutor.

Though irked and irritated, Shantanu tried as much as he could to convince her. He talked of convention and practical wisdom, which only outraged Satyavati. She would not change her decision.

"You don't want to send your son to an ashrama. But that won't be good for your son."

"I know what is good for my son and what is not,"

Satyawati hissed back.

Shantanu had no strength to hit back. Ganga's absence from his life had left him feeble in spirit. He was weakened both physically and mentally. He knew Satyavati was driven by her base selfish desires. But she was his wife and he could not drop her at a mere hint. A child was at the root of his dispute with both Ganga and Satyavati. In the first case it was the life of a child that triggered the dispute and now it was his education.

Shantanu continued to try to convince Satyavati. He said, "at the ashrama, the teacher is the master, mentor and guardian. There, he is in his element, awake and sublime."

Satyavati would not yield. "If the scriptures can enlighten a learner at an ashrama, they can do the same at the palace," was her point of view. She stressed that "even while receiving instructions from his mentor, my son must not forget that he himself is the master and his trainer was a mere state official. I am not bothered about any sublimity arising from the instruction. I want my son to know that he is the king and the master."

"Satyavati!" Shantanu all but exploded. "Learning and enlightenment, arts and skills, contemplation and meditation, arms and scriptures-all these were created by our rishis to make man godlike and not a total beast... And the teacher who instructs your son as a state official will not be awe-inspiring but subdued. He will acquire an inferiority complex and a tendency to earn money. He will make no distinction between the just and unjust, fair and foul, and righteous and unrighteous. He will enhance not wisdom but pride."

Satyavati did not seem impressed. Shantanu was reminded that she was trained and qualified by her father and much could not be expected of her. It was the same father-daughter duo who had felt no remorse in stripping Bhishma of his legitimate rights. But a father and a husband are two separate entities. A woman is often gratified in seconding her father and defying her husband. The husband is her closest friend and also her bitterest foe. A woman who subdues her husband finds herself liberated from all laws. That is what Ganga did and what Satyavati also wanted to do.

Then Shantanu thought of Bhishma who was keeping aloof from all administrative jobs. He could be an ideal mentor and teacher, Shantanu decided and briefed her so. A hornet's nest was stirred. Nothing could be more outrageous to Satyavati who rejected the very idea outright as she would never believe and trust Bhishma in this respect as she herself had deprived him of his rights. That Bhishma would retaliate was a foregone conclusion in her mind.

Shantanu tried to correct her perception. "Bhishma is not that sort. You have failed to understand him."

"Even an ant would not spare one who has robbed its food whereas Bhishma is a man. I have seen fishermen kill each other over a load of fish."

"Satyavati! You have only seen fishermen and not kshatriya princes who sacrifice their lives defending the weak. You were brought up among the lower ones and that does not mean that the world is without the higher category of people."

"We are poor, and so we are inferior," Satyavati was visibly hurt.

"Poverty does not mean inferiority. Even the sages are poor. I refer to our values. A man is superior by his conduct, and his conduct is backed by his values. Mind Bhishma's conduct. The Kuru kingdom is insignificant to him. The earthly pleasures have no import for him. And you think he will take his revenge on your son, his own brother?"

"Say whatever you may, but in this matter, I will rely on my wisdom. And I have decided that I will not concede the responsibility of training my son to Bhishma, who is the greatest threat to him."

"As you wish, Satyavati!" said Shantanu suppressing his rage. "As for me, I will assume that a good guru was not destined for thy son. I don't want any debate with you. The decision will be yours. But, I have some points for you to ponder. Would you care to listen?"

"Bhishma is not a man. He is a god," declared Shantanu to a reluctant Satyavati. "Though his father, I regard him no less than a great man. He has nothing to lose now. The world is only to gain from him."

"Then, listen to this," said Satyavati defiantly. "Even if I approve of your statements, I will still keep my sons at a distance from him."

"Why?" Shantanu was amazed.

"Because I will not have my sons as renunciants like Bhishma who could be easily divested of his possessions. I want my sons to be princes and not recluses. Let them not abdicate their authority but fight for it till end. This world belongs to fighters. I will not appoint Bhishma, a coward, as my son's guru."

"I was told that a woman symbolises compassion, mercy and kindness," Shantanu muttered.

"I am not that sort of a woman. And I am not inclined to embrace such an ideal as would make me vulnerable to befooling. You must have also heard that a woman is both passion and illusion. She desires gratification and the right to gratify herself. I desire wealth and power and glory-everything. I am the queen of the Kuru dynasty and also aspire to be the mother of the king of Hastinapur. I don't relish talks of spirituality, sacrifice and renunciation, and I wish my sons to be like that."

There was nothing more to say after her candid confession about herself.

"If that is your wish," said Shantanu, "Bhishma will not instruct your sons. They will not be admitted to any ashrama. They will be trained at the royal palace. And some brahmin under the royal patronage will be their guru."

Satyavati was somewhat appeased. "I won't leave my sons to be unduly exposed to the sages' influence. Rather, I believe that if Bhishma had not been left in the ashramas as a child, he would not be so detached from worldly pleasures as he is. Therefore, I don't want my sons to be in close contact with him."

"That will also be taken care of," said Shantanu and left the chamber.

Sleep eluded Shantanu till late that night. At one time he had resisted Bhishma's dispassionateness and magnanimity, which he had attributed to his tender age. But, now the mist had dispersed. Bhishma was definitely happier than him for he had forsaken desire which he, King Shantanu, himself had not been able to do.

Shantanu was already puzzled at Ganga's demeanour, and now here was Satyavati. Ganga deserted him when he wanted Devavrata to himself. And now here was Satyavati, his second wife, who was out to deprive him of his first child? Can a woman be like that? Satyavati was not even prepared to listen and understand. She wanted to cut the very arms that would protect her sons.

And she was there by Shantanu's will. He had brought her. Shantanu himself had placed fire in the foundation of his home so that it might be burnt down. But would he be able to abandon Satyavati now, even if he so wished? He was so blindly, so unwisely passionate! Nature had awarded frailty to an otherwise strong and able man! He was incapacitated by his foolish attachment.

11

A vast vacuity stared Bhishma in the face.

His conduct, his vow and his sacrifice had been widely acclaimed. Rama's fourteen year abdication for his father Dasaratha exalted him as an incarnation of God. But Bhishma withdrew himself from the kingdom for good, which was no mean achievement. Why this vast vacuity then? He should rather have felt fulfilled.

Was Bhishma regretting his decision?

It was a moment of introspection for him. He found no trace of regret. His vow was not taken in the heat of the moment that he would regret in the calmer moments. He would take the same vow if a similar moment arose. This vow and this sacrifice had rendered a sublimity to his existence. He could not ignore the truth that a sacrifice elevates a man to higher levels. His deed had made him even greater than his father. So far he had been honoured for his princedom; but now he was honoured even as an individual by the wizened ministers and the aged senapatis (commanders). In a way, he had overgrown his age, demolished the divisions of time. And from there ensued a sense of futility.

Bhishma was young and a long life awaited him. But what would he do with that long life? Granted that the rishis aspired to live for a hundred years. But why? Why would he require that longevity? For enjoyment? For acquisitions? For expansion? For protection? For sacrifice?

For charity? For self-enhancement? It was absurd. He had no enjoyment on his mind now. He had forsaken even the lust for a woman, the essential and highest form of enjoyment. He had let go of the very kingdom of the Kurus. So what could attract him now? It was no more his kingdom and his subjects. Who should he look after and who should he protect? These were not his people.

Bhishma was confounded-whether the mist had cleared or everything was blurred. When all enjoyment wasted the body, why should a man in the first place go for them? When all was to be renounced, why acquire it in the first place? Does it mean you acted against your own goals? What was Nature's expectation from man? That he should take birth and be fascinated by this illusion and prepare to achieve it and be successful in that. Then one day he would realise that the things were where they had been, only his grip was slackening. That his organs were gradually deteriorating and causing him pain. It was his mind that would not yield and would go on yearning for more. Even the failing senses would be no deterrent; he would either crave for the next birth or extend his enjoyments through his progeny, and Nature would support him in the Name of tradition.

But in Bhishma's case, even that would not work-as he was not going to have any descendants; there would not be any tradition or rebirth for Bhishma.

What would Bhishma do? His person and life were meaningless to him. But suicide was sin. He must live on. Why? The tenets of dharma, artha, kama, moksha were not for him. And moksha (emancipation) was attainable through observing the dharma (duty). But what was Bhishma's dharma? Was it to be different from other men's dharma? Was dharma common to all? Or each of us should discover his or her own dharma?

King Shantanu was enamoured of the boatman's daughter; his dharma was to wed her... for he wanted more sons for the continuity of his dynasty, for the protection of his kingdom. And it was the dharma of Satyavati's father to ensure the rights of his daughter and her children; that was exactly what he had done. Why then, should it be Bhishma's dharma to forgo his own rights? As a son, his dharma was to renounce. As an individual, though, his dharma was to defend his own right. Was he first a son or an individual?

The point of rights had returned with its pressing preponderance to him. Who would he confront to claim his rights? His father? His yet unborn brothers? What had Bhishma lost? What were his wants? What new pleasures could he expect?

There it occurred to Bhishma that he had no grievances, no malice against anyone... against his father, his mother or against anyone else. He was intensely relieved. A certain bliss seeped into him and overwhelmed his very existence.

A burden was lifted off his chest. His father was happy to have Satyavati. His mother was happy to have secured the assurance of a kingdom for her children to come. Bhishma was greatly gratified. There was nothing else he desired for himself.

Presently, he desired to see his parents for he had not been there for quite some time.

Bhishma was denied admittance to Satyavati's chamber. The maids told him that the queen was indisposed and did not wish to see anyone. He made a few enquiries and returned disappointed and contemplating the strange writ of destiny. Mother Ganga had disposed of Bhishma's seven elder brothers and Bhishma was shorn of all attachment and desires so that mother Satyavati's first son would be the prince and eventually the king of Hastinapur. If all that was predestined, how could Ganga's eight sons have survived?

The first thing Shantanu did on his return to the palace

at eventide was to see Satyavati.

"How are you, Satya?"

"I'm fine! How was your day?"

Shantanu complained of his fatigue. He attributed it to the fact that he was left all alone to look after the administrative responsibilities, with Bhishma keeping aloof, which was due to the prevailing circumstances. If Bhishma was inclined to seek knowledge and wisdom, it was but natural.

Satyavati was obviously irritated when Bhishma's name was mentioned. She was quite defiant in admitting that he was not and would not be allowed to see her. She even asked Shantanu to tell Bhishma that she was not interested in seeing him and, therefore, he should better not come to her palace.

Shantanu tried to ask her about Bhishma's fault but was rudely silenced."Fault or no fault, I don't want any debate. I just don't want to meet him." She added that, "My son Chitrangada should be consecrated as the heir apparent so that the subjects and Bhishma know who was the prince of Hastinapur."

"Your will shall be done," Shantanu blurted out.

12

Shantanu sat in his official chamber, listening to informants from diverse regions. It was a usually routine affair until a reluctant messenger, upon being granted amnesty, divulged something that had the potential to startle and alarm the king.

"O Great King!" said the man. "Prince Bhishma has built a cottage on the banks of the Ganga, where he spends most of his time."

Initially Shantanu dismissed the news as trivial and insignificant. What if Bhishma has built himself a cottage? The whole land is his. He, if he so desires, can raise a town of palaces. Or was the man, on behalf of Satyavati, accusing Bhishma of usurping Chitrangada's land? But why should Bhishma need to do that? Shantanu mused.

Then, as an afterthought, he asked the man, "what does Bhishma do at the cottage?"

"Contemplation and meditation."

That was a real fuel to stoke the fire of concern in Shantanu's bosom. Contemplation and meditation at this age? Was Bhishma heading for the vanaprastha (the stage of renunciation)?

Shantanu felt a sense of guilt that pricked his conscience. Wasn't it the right option for Bhishma for whom the stage of brahmacharya (celibacy) had elapsed and whose household life he had dedicated to him, his father?

How could Shantanu indict Bhishma, who was doing

nothing wrong and who was universally extolled even at his tender age? Shantanu would rather castigate himself. He had once saved Devavrata from the murderous clutches of Ganga, at the cost of her wrath, and reared him to youth. Now he had offered the same Devavrata back to Ganga, where he had devoted himself to contemplation and meditation!

Shantanu decided that Bhishma's reclusion was not going to do anyone any good. It won't be in the interest of either the ruler, Shantanu, or the ruled. And he felt it was not good even for Satyavati and her sons Chitrangada and Vichitravirya.

Shantanu realised that he was being driven by a heartache for his son Bhishma. It was in man's nature to avoid treading the path of universal ideals. Moreover, he took no pleasure in having his dear ones attempt the same. Dashratha was not pleased at his son's exile. The pain caused by his son Rama's sacrifice cost Dashratha his life. Although Shantanu was all praise for Bhishma's sacrifice but his reclusion would never be appreciated by him. That way Satyavati had been wiser in declaring that she would never encourage her sons' proximity to Bhishma.

Shantanu thought of persuading Bhishma to regain his princedom. All was still not lost. The ground could still be recovered. However, it was virtually impossible for Bhishma, or for anyone for that matter, to remain still or go back to his former position. Could an arrow change its trajectory midway and return to its quiver? And why should Bhishma return, even if requested by his father, and agree to marry? And would that be acceptable to Satyavati?

Even as Shantanu weighed the pros and cons, the aged minister Vishnudutt came to meet him to express his concern. Shantanu tried to quell his fears and asked him to make the chariot ready.

With no specific destination in his mind, Shantanu mounted the chariot. Such despondence was nothing new to the king's character. The minister at once knew the king needed rest. He asked where the king would like to go and, accordingly, drove him to Queen Satyavati's palace.

Satyavati did not seem pleased at the king's presence. During the ensuing dialogue she revealed that the ten-year-old 'prince' Chitrangada had been out for excursion and that he flogged the charioteer for not taking the vehicle he rode into the royal park which, as the charioteer submitted, was to be navigated on foot.

Shantanu was intensely hurt to hear that. The charioteer and other royal staff were all quite older than that ten-year-old wanton lad, who acted as a prince and punished anyone for any imagined guilt. So that was the conduct of manners taught by the teachers and trainers appointed by Satyavati. Shantanu was peeved to ruminate.

When asked for further details, Satyawati fumed.

"What would happen?" she said, "before anything could happen, your old man Vishnudutt arrived on the scene and started investigating as though he were some royal staff having more authority than the prince. Instead of chastising the driver, the old man favoured him and declared that he was right in his submission that chariots were not allowed inside the royal park. The prince was enraged but, regarding the minister's old age, he did not flog him and simply hit him with his tiny hand before leaving the place with a warning that he would complain against the minister and the charioteer to the king."

Shantanu was all pity for Satyavati. She was so overwhelmed by her love for her son and the import of his princely status that her conscience had failed her. She had overlooked that it was the prince among the three who was the real culprit. None but Chitrangada deserved the punishment. He was so blinded by his princedom that he recognised no barriers to his powers, and regarded no rules, constraints and moral bindings.

Shantanu tried to convince Satyavati that there were rules of constraint for princes too, while she sat there speechless, staring wide-eyed at him in wonder and rage. Then he stood up without any further arguments and left. Wisdom did not call for any comments about Bhishma.

13

Bhishma was engaged with certain strange feelings.

Life in a palace was altogether different. It inevitably evoked a contrast with other palaces. Whereas in the cottage, he never compared it with other cottages in terms of space or extent. Did it all depend on how one felt about it? If procurement was considered a measure of greatness, one would be gratified even if depriving others. Whereas, if one considered renunciation the criterion of sublimity, one would be exalted in even renouncing all. The self was primary; satisfying the self was essential to happiness. Pride in any form would lead to downfall. So pride must be gotten rid of. But for that, first the mind must be freed of all pride, and for that, craving must be abolished; greed must be shed.

Bhishma proceeded to compare the life of a king with that of a recluse. A king had everything but peace. In his state of disquiet, he would take to war, hunting, gambling and wedding. Whereas a recluse, though destitute, would never crave for a piece of land; even as a forest dwelling creature, he would never think of hunting; even amidst penury, he would never be inclined to gambling; and even without a woman, he would never desire one. The more one possessed, the more one craved. Does our longing for something increase as it gets closer to our grasp? Was it because of this that kings raised towns and recluses abandoned them for the woods, where there were no comparisons, no likings, no greed and no craving.

If Bhishma had been a prince, he would most likely have become a king. He would then have performed yajnas (sacrificial rites and rituals), organised an army, prepared for wars. But now, as he did not have a kingdom, there was no question of its expansion. How happy he was! There was only commitment and no liking and therefore, no greed.

Bhishma's thoughts were disrupted by the entry of Ashvasena, the king's charioteer. With due regards and greetings, Bhishma asked him the reason of his visit. When Ashvasena told him that he had brought the chariot to fetch him on the king's wish to see him, Bhishma could not decline.

Shantanu greeted Bhishma warmly. "Come my son," he said, "these days you can be seen only when summoned specifically!"

Bhishma could recognise a tinge of complaint in his father's voice which he admitted as quite warranted, for he had not been to his palace in recent times. His father declared that Bhishma was no longer attached to him, which was quite untrue, and enquired why he refrained from seeing him and avoided him.

What could Bhishma say? Was his father not aware that once in mother Satyavati's presence, Bhishma had realised that he was not welcome there? And Bhishma never relished it. In fact, he never wanted to come between his father and mother. It was actually to save his father from any unsavory situation, any disgrace, that he was trying to cut himself from his father, the entire royal family, the entire kingdom. However, he could not disclose it to his father who could take it otherwise.

Anyway, he had never harboured any antipathy towards his father whose life, he knew, had been a puppet in the hands of destiny. His kingdom brought him no happiness. His accomplishments caused him only afflictions. The pleasures he had derived in this old age from his extremely beautiful wife, Satyavati, were acutely belittled by the discomforts and hassles accompanying it. His two sons had given him more pain than pleasure.

"I got some news about you that should have gladdened me... My son, you facilitated my marriage, gave me a new household, and steered clear of my way so that I would have no sense of responsibility for and no guilt about you. And now that you are on your way to spiritual enhancement, you are getting more capable."

"How, sire?" Bhishma was curious.

"Giving up is greater than getting! One who gives up is more capable than the one who gets. At this age, you could have been considered capable with all your martial exploits, but your renunciation of all regal accomplishments and the shaping up of a new personality manifests an even more capable man. Frankly speaking, I now realise that with you as my only son, I was not only the father of a son but the father of a hundred sons. Though I now have Chitrangada and Vichitravirya, I have them at your cost. I have lost you in the bargain ... They are the sort that makes a father childless. As you might have heard, Chitrangada is gaining fame as a haughty and hot-tempered youngster. At this immature age of fourteen, he incenses, challenges and provokes anyone. I fear he might be killed in a duel someday."

Bhishma contradicted his father, saying that there was no likelihood of Chitrangada being killed in that manner, and even if that happened, it would be a hero's death, which was only creditable for a kshatriya.

"It won't be a hero's death. Getting killed as a punishment for shedding blood is a bandit's dismissal... And that twelve-year-old Vichitravirya! He is dangerously licentious."

"Why don't you check them?"

"I am not authorised."

"Why?"

"That's fate's another prank on me, my son! Ganga's sons were hers only, none of them except you could be Shantanu's son. Similarly, Satyavati's sons are exclusively hers, not Shantanu's who has myriad liabilities and duties towards them but no right over them."

"Don't say that!"

"It's true, my son! Satyavati would not allow any restraints on them. They are princes and they can't be restrained is what she believes, otherwise they lose their vigour. They have to consider themselves above other men. She stresses and argues that they have the right to punish and intimidate whosoever they would."

"Are they beyond all admonition?"

"All, my son. You won't believe me if I declare that I have got scared of her now. What I have come to believe is that since she is from a poor family, the ghost of poverty won't leave her. The fear of reverting to her former state so haunts her that she becomes abnormal. She needs but the slightest excuse to conclude that I am seeking to abandon her, to debar her sons from the princely rights. She is categorical in her accusation that since she is from a poor family with no regal backing, I am torturing her and that I am so sensual that no woman would live with me, that I expelled Ganga and rumoured that she deserted me... yes Bhishma, if you listen to her bickering, you would believe I am really as bad as she announces."

"Is she that wicked?"

"She is evil. Her evil has warped her thinking... She targets only me. She doubts and distrusts me the most. I even contemplate at times to desert her or leave this place... But I can't do that. That would become another reason for my subjects to think low of me. They will see her wailing and shouting in streets and judge me the way Chitrangada and Vichitravirya do now. In fact, the two of them stare at me as if asking why I was harassing their mother. I can't endure that."

Bhishma condemned himself for having hurled his father into such an abyss of misery. He decided he had no right to congratulate himself for his unique sacrifice to bring happiness to him, whereas he had only worsened his life. That was an unpardonable sin, he thought.

"No doubt I will be free if I decide to abandon her, but then Chitrangada and Vichitravirya will be left to her mercy. There will be no bridle on whatever she would like to do to them. She will treat them anyway she liked. After all, they are my sons. I cannot leave them at the mercy of that morbid woman. It could be disastrous for them... Moreover, a sick person is supposed to be looked after. She cannot be left, not in the present state at least."

"Which means there is no redemption, sire?"

"No son, none. Nature is the supreme judge and a judge could be harsh too. Everyone must pay for their sins and that is exactly what I am doing."

Their dialogue concluded with Shantanu exhorting Bhishma to usurp the kingdom which he, understandably, declined.

"If I break my oath, not only will I break the oath, the citadel of the Kurus' fame will also collapse. I am sorry I cannot uphold the glory of being an obedient son," said Bhishma and left with a reverent bow.

Shantanu watched Bhishma as if the very sublimity of the Kuru dynasty was retiring from the palace.

14

Satyavati was curious to know the purpose of Bhishma's visit. The malice that lurked behind her query was all too visible. She had in the past registered her protest against Bhishma seeing Chitrangada and Vichitravirya, which had hurt Shantanu, and he had not been able to convince her that such rancorous antagonism for Bhishma would do her no good.

For her, Bhishma was only Shantanu's son and not hers, and he was no brother to Chitrangada and Vichitravirya. Now, she wanted to alienate Bhishma from his father too.

Restricted by the possibility of Satyavati's anger flaring up and their clash getting exposed, Shantanu maintained utmost calm. But he knew that Satyavati's sleuths would divulge the details of the father-son dialogue if he didn't. Above all he feared her temper.

The ensuing altercation bared Shantanu's fiercest side, that which scared even Satyavati, who was readily subdued.

"What's wrong with you? Are you all right?" she said. "I just asked why did you call Bhishma. Stillif you don't want to tell me, it's all right. Let it be."

Even in his agitation, Shantanu could see how shaken Satyavati was. He knew Satyavati wished him to herself alone, cut off from all, and hale and hearty, to be the implement of her authority.

He pronounced that he was not worried about himself, nor for her, but his sole concern was his two sons-

Chitrangada and Vichitravirya.

Shantanu's doubt in the two princes' efficacy tampered her spirit. When he disclosed that he wished to put them under Bhishma's mentorial tutelage, the mere mention of Bhishma's name was enough to offend her. The so far timid and discomfited woman was in a jiffy transformed into a ferocious lioness, ready to pounce upon him, her claws and teeth eager to tear into his flesh ruthlessly.

"Righteousness is vanished from this earth," the lioness roared. "The earth is reduced to a hell now. How do we trust anyone! Better the earth is broken asunder, the sky burst open, the sea swallow, and the fire raze this earth. Let this be a great land of death, death, death!"

Shantanu feared she would go mad.

"Satyavati!" Shantanu caught her by hand. "What's wrong with you?"

"What's wrong with me?" Satyavati jerked herself off. "The universal king of the Kuru dynasty has forgotten his promises, rather he is withdrawing from them."

When, understandably irked, Shantanu denied any such promises, Satyavati hissed, "Now you may even deny our marriage....that Chitrangada and Vichitravirya are not your sons."

She was particularly baffled by the scary prospect of Bhishma holding the reins from the backstage, that he would run the kingdom even as her own son would be the king.

Shantanu tried his best to convince Satyawati that he would in no way interfere in their matters. He warned her that if even after his death she continued to be hostile to Bhishma, only she would be responsible for the downfall of the kingdom of Hastinapur.

Those were his parting words.

15

After crossing the Ganga, when Bhishma reached his cottage, he could not make out if he was more in grief or in astonishment. He had sacrificed his life's pleasures to realise his father's wish, to allow him his life's greatest pleasure. But somehow that happiness was converted to extreme misery and affliction. How does it happen that a man creates a garden and it growsinto a den of ferocious beasts.

The more he thought about it, the more confused he became. The frequently tormenting riddle was once more rearing its head. Did a man's conscience, his judgement and his action have no meaning on their own? Shantanu, and even Bhishma himself, had decided that Satyavati would bring utmost bliss to the king's life. But the consequence was very different. In fact, the consequence was the truth. A man's desire was not the truth. The desire often deluded him. It was not grounded in his conscience. His father's agony had compelled Bhishma to work for realisation of his desire. He had then not cared to examine whether his father's desire was judicious or otherwise. It was only Nature's conduct, the creator's desire, that was judicious. Man was selfish. With his limited intellect he thinks only of his happiness and grief. Nature was concerned with the whole creation's happiness and grief. Only those who were generous and broad minded can come close to Nature.

Narrowness and self were yet another name of folly. Devavrata ought to have considered that Nature had planned the attraction between man and woman so that they could procreate. It was not a means to enjoy arousal and excitement. Nature endorsed union between the couple of the same age, so that they would produce children and rear them. Satyavati's father preferred wealth, and King Shantanu the urge of flesh. And Devavrata had imposed his own desire on Nature, and the consequence was there to see. The three were cheated by their intellect.

Nature is straightforward in her justice. If milk is added to water, it dissolves and loses its entity. If butter is added to water, it floats on the surface and does not dissolve but retains its separate character. Devavrata had mixed the milk of his desire with Nature's stream. He had not changed it through piety and wisdom to produce butter.

Andonce again his father was expressing another desire. Guided again by his paternal fondness, he was inclined to delegate the kingdom of Kuru to Bhishma. Shantanu was biased by his attachment for Bhishma. But should Bhishma give in to his whim and rush in to do his desire? Would that not be another blunder? A descendent of Kuru, should he crave for kingdom? Violate his own pledge? Reverse his own promise? Should he surrender his own desire to his father'? Bhishma was in a quandary.

There were hordes and hordes of questions pestering him. What was the truth? The dharma? What was his duty? He was incapacitated, not able to decide. And in that state, he knew he should do what came in as a duty to him. Decision was possibly not in his hands, and dharma was still not within his comprehension.

16

King Shantanu's private chamber was thronged with an unprecedented number of people.

The king was on his bed. Queen Satyavati sat close to its head. The aged minister and the official priest stood in the front. Chitrangada and Vichitravirya sat beside their mother. Then there was a team of the official physicians, complete with assistants and attendants, and maids and male servants waiting for any orders.

Shantanu, however, appeared oblivious of their presence. He would open his eyes, look around in anticipation, and was dismayed at Bhishma's absence.

When offered a potion, he declined it saying he did not need any medicine but wanted to see Devavrata. Satyavati was the most alarmed. The king wanted to see Devavrata! Would he declare him the heir? What if he did that? Would that mean Chitrangada was going to be deprived of the throne? That Satyavati was going to be reverted to her former position of a Nishada woman?

Assured of Bhishma's arrival, King Shantanu eventually received the medicine and called for the rites. He was, in his moments of retrospection, concerned about Satyavati, short of forty now, who had a long, difficult life before her, and her two innocent sons to take care of.

His pragmatism cautioned Shantanu. He was not to be deceived by appearance. He knew that a lot of people who now appeared so affable and amiable would spare no time taking the garb of wolves when he had closed his eyes. He knew that the potential and prospect of the throne could not only arouse the beast dormant in a man but also activate it. A man is transformed as the possibility of achieving the throne nears: horns appear on his head, his jaws become bloody, nails sharp, and he grows an insatiable thirst for blood. After his demise, Satyavati's own people would turn against her. Her sons could be assassinated. She herself could be killed, abdicated or enslaved or even forced into begging. Anything was possible. She was still so beautiful that any king would complement himself on having her as his consort.

But was Shantanu still enamoured of Satyavati? Would he yearn for yet another life with her as his wife? What was his gain in this life? What was it that provided him only happiness and no woe, no pain? Was it kingdom? Wife? Children? Wealth? Regal power? Nothing. Yet Shantanu would not say 'no'.

"Devavrata!" He tried to pronounce in delirium. Satyavati hurried forward, and so did Chitrangada, the minister and the priest.

'Devavrata!' Shantanu whispered to himself. 'You will rear them. The two boys are immature and Satyavati is ignorant. You have to shield your two brothers against her ruinous influence.'

He felt Devavrata was listening.

Then his eyes opened and he saw Bhishma leaning on him. He tried to utter something but the words were lost on him. Then he closed his eyes forever.

Satyavati was horribly shaken. What if Bhishma declared himself king? Would she be able to confront him? She had no military support. Would the boatmen come to her rescue and deliver the needful with their boats, oars, nets and baskets? Her Baba had no chariots, horses, bows and arrows, and submissive soldiers.

Satyavati was afraid of what future held for her after Shantanu's death. Where should she go, whom to approach for justice? The vital question boomeranged on her.

She swooned, and was held, just before she would hit the floor, by Bhishma.

"Mother!" he called, "Mother! Have patience. Bhishma will do anything to alleviate your troubles."

But he was intercepted by Chitrangada, who rushed forward to his mother's side as if to free her from Bhishma's clutches. "You need not bother," said he rudely to Bhishma. "What if father is no more, I am still there. I will look after my mother. Your help is not solicited."

Bhishma was momentarily stunned, though he managed to mutter, "I just forgot you are grown up now." And he persuaded himself to honour the need of the occasion and stay put there.

It was a moment of revival for Satyavati. She witnessed with elation how her own son, Chitrangada, had not only succoured her but even shoved Bhishma aside. Bhishma might have treated him as a kid, but he was not. After all, he was the son of the mighty King Shantanu. A lion's cub was naturally endowed with his attributes.

So Satyavati had so far under-estimated Chitrangada. She was scared that Bhishma would lift and throw her by the Ganga. But Chitrangada displayed his valour and Bhishma was forced back into his timidity. Now Chitrangada was not a prince, but a king who not only Bhishma but all must fear. A king's power was his authority to punish.

She was reassured. She regained her elan. Marrying the king was merely a small step towards a big goal. Her conjugal life was just an occasion to wait for the end of the journey, which she had attained now. Her goal had been to see herself as the Queen Mother... and it was a moment of triumph, not deprivation. Enthused by her new-found vigour, she commanded the mahamantri (Prime Minister) to arrange for the king's funeral rites.

After a long time now did Satyavati feel relieved in ernest. She could comfortably ignore Bhishma, his predominance.

17

Mahamantri Vishnudutt approached Bhishma at his cottage. His talks revealed his dignity was sorely hurt. He was distraught and dejected.

Was he in distress? Bhishma wondered and wanted to know.

What else was there in Hastinapur, the Mahamantri complained, and Bhishma was startled. What about the common people then, he could only guess.

"When you had established this ashram, I was really bothered," the mahamantri said. "But, now I think you had best guessed the things to come in future. Better than sitting in the assembly at Hastinapur is to retire to the woods and make a cottage beside the river or go to the Himalayas to do penance."

"Mahamantri! It is considered a great honour to be accommodated in the assembly at Hastinapur," Bhishma offered to disagree.

"No, respected sir! It is not so now. To abuse an aged minister, an ascetic brahmin, a scholar, a well-wisher, or a gallant warrior and to intimidate one in the assembly is nothing unusual for the new king."

"Isn't the king inclined to veneration?"

"The king is interested in only insulting others. He is the only king ever occupying the throne of Hastinapur who has taken a vow to insult each and every councillor."

"What about the Acharya?"

"Depending on the state stipends, what can a brahmin, an ordinary state worker, do? He has no say in the administration."

"And the royal priest?"

"He is planning to leave Hastinapur."

Bhishma was stunned. So all was not well in Hastinapur. But the queen mother, did she exercise no control over the king?

"She believes that the king must behave like a king and the people have to honour the king's will."

The prime minister proposed to resign.

"You say the king is not so thoughtful. In that case, he deserves the benefit of prime minister Vishnudutt's wisdom and experience."

"Frankly, how often have you visited Hastinapur after King Shantanu's last rites?" The prime minister wanted to know.

"Never. Because I wish to be away from the affairs of the state."

"Would you do the same if the queen mother had, after the king's demise, urged you to take charge of your two little brothers?"

Bhishma had no ready answer to that. Rather he tried to avert it. The prime minister was apt to remind him of his duty and informed him of the neighbouring states that had turned hostile. In fact, Chitrangada had antagonised not only the kshatriya rulers but the Nagas, the Yakshas, the Gandharvas, the Kinnars and the Rakshakas as well. They are getting organised against Hastinapur."

"Is the queen mother aware of that?"

"She is a mother and no stateswoman. She honours the universality of the king of Hastinapur's militant exploits."

"Truly, it is a fact that war and game have been the kshatriya's sport."

"Then truly also, sport even causes one's downfall and assassination."

"Do you fear that?"

"Besides there are two bits of information for you. First several Kuru chiefs are planning to meet you to convey that King Chitrangada was going beyond limits of endurance and it posed a threat of insurgency. They want to request you to assume power before some other clan puts an end to this rule. Another development concerns the Gandharva troops that have already approached Kurukshetra which, you know, is not so far from Hastinapur. The kings of the Gandharvas and Hastinapur are likely to be pressed into a chariot combat. Only God knows what would happen."

And Prime Minister Vishnudutt left Bhishma in contemplation.

Bhishma knew that under the prevailing circumstances a combat could be fatal. He knew there was no one who could or would sacrifice his life for a king who never loved anyone. However, Bhishma was bound and crippled by his vow.

Gradually, he calmed down.

18

The messenger seemed to have arrived in haste. He rushed in, panting and puffing. Observing no formalities, no etiquettes.

Satyavati eyed him scrupulously. Her conceit hadmelted. She was now not a queen, the queen mother, or a member of the royal family. A sheer mother she was, whose son had marched to Kurukshetra to take on the Gandharva king in a chariot combat.

As the messenger fumbled for words, Satyavati commanded him to speak out. She had been anticipating the worst, though she tried to hoodwink herself by thinking that her son might not have been necessarily... he might have rather been defeated, or captured, or injured, or the man might have arrived with some other news. But the worst had actually happened. Chitrangada, the king of Hastinapur, had met a hero's fate, the man said.

Satyavati had no words to respond. Her fate had betrayed her on crucial points. The man she sincerely loved was abandoned by her. She had but an illegitimate son, who was now growing up at sage Parashar'sashram and had already earned himself an enviable repute and veneration as a great rishi; she couldn'tcall him her own. And the man she wedded, though old, was also wrested away by the design of the providence. And now it was Chitrangada. What else was in store for her!

She wailed out inconsolably. The cue was instantly

picked and the palace soon echoed with wails and whines from other inmates.

What was left for her now? Vichitravirya! A tender weakling of twelve, squarely unlike his brother, he was never visited by any thoughts of aggression. He shied away from fights and never remembered that th sword on his waist was not hung as a decorative piece. His hours were comfortably consumed in the company of courtly maids.

Whereas, after King Shantanu's demise, Chitrangada had been gutsy enough to confront Bhishma, Vichitravirya could not even stand erect before him. Would he be able to defend his mother?

Satyavati found herself in a fix. If Bhishma, as pressed by the gentry, chose to assume office, who would prevent him from marrying? And, if he did, would his powerful consort from some mighty royal family tolerate Satyavati, a mere boatman's daughter, in the palace? Would the new queen let Vichitravirya, an obstacle in her own son's princedom, survive? Wasn't it exactly what Satyavati had done to Bhishma? So there was no escape for Satyavati! She even contemplated fleeing the state.

If that was her fate consequent upon marrying the aged king that she should have to think of escape to save herself and her son, what was wrong about Parashar? Won't she have been happy with her recluse and their children at the ashram? She had bartered her happiness for a splendid royal life. And now she was faced with the prospect of quitting that life for good.

It was amidst those moments of emotional upheaval that she was informed of the mahamantri and the acharya's visit. It was a formal call which would not interest her now. But, before she could refuse to see them, they were already in.

The acharya intimated her that in that hour of grief, they were faced with an impending danger. He warned that the army of Hastinapur, which had failed to stall the Gandharvaraja at Kurukshetra even while King Shantanu was alive, would by no means be able to do that now in Hastinapur, now that the king was no more there. The only option in that case would be to open the gates for him and let the people be on his mercy.

"No," she bellowed. It was Bhishma alone that occupied her mind as the one and only enemy, who could do her utmost harm. In her preoccupation, she had sinisterly ignored the real danger lurking over her and the kingdom, in the form of the Gandharva king who had already defeated and killed her son Chitrangada.

"Mother queen," the prime minister said, "to defend the state is our prime duty. And, therefore, even in this hour of grief, we cannot indulge in sloth. We must buckle our armour, otherwise not only the Gandharaja but also the Panchalas and the Matsyas are waiting in the wings with their sinister engagement on our borders."

The only way out of the dilemma was to invite Bhishma, the minister suggested.

Would the army of Hastinapur potentially defeat the Gandharvaraja, Satyavati doubted.

"Mother queen," the minister proposed, "the moment he arrives in Hastinapur, the Gandharva king will not take a moment to cross back through the hills and seek refuge in his kingdom like a frightened mouse that hides into its hole upon encountering a mighty enemy. And the Panchalas and the Matryas will have no guts to come out of their kingdom."

Satyavati's thoughts raced. It was going to be a crucial decision with far-reaching impacts. If Bhishma did arrive and the kingdom was saved, she could get rid of him otherwise. But if she did not call Bhishma and the Gandharvaraja intruded into Hastinapur, the Gandharva king could kill her and Vichitravirya as he had done to Chitrangada.

Satyavati eventually acquiesced.

"Go, mahamantri, and you too acharya. Go and tell Bhishma that I call him," she ordered, still doubtful of the prudence of her decision.

She condemned herself for using Bhishma's vow as a sword to keep him off Hastinapur whereas she should have made it a shield to counter the attacks from the enemy. 'You have committed a blunder, Satyavati,' she chastised herself. 'You should have utilised the fact of being the wife of Bhishma's father as a right to put Bhishma in a bond. Bhishma could have been bound with that cord.' She should have questioned the minister about her own and her son's fate post Bhishma's entry.

Anyway there was no time for that now. She had to brace herself for whatever was to come her way.

19

Bhishma, in compliance with Satyavati's wish, presented himself before her.

She noticed that it was a different Bhishma arriving on Chitrangada's demise from the one who had departed from Hastinapur after Shantanu's death. The earlier Bhishma was a prince- determined, capable, a fighter, and equipped with authority whereas this one was a recluse- dispassionate, feeble, and endowed with dreamy eyes. This Bhishma aroused no fear in her. This was the same one who had renounced all worldly and royal comforts and pleasures, for her sake, and had with all humility begged her to 'come to Hastinapur.'

The very next moment she cautioned herself. She was being the same sillySatyavati who had been swept by Parashar off her feet in love. It was thanks to her father's prudence that she was not stuck in that position for good; without it she could never attain the status she was enjoying now. Should she succumb to the same silly sentiment now by anointing Bhishma as the crown prince and submit Vichitravirya into his serfdom forever! No.

She tried to catch Bhishma on the wrong foot, complaining that he was still harbouring his 'anger' even after Chitrangada was dead following his battle with the Gandharvas for three years in a row. "You don't get formally invited to an event of bereavement and death, my son," she complained.

Bhishma's conscience advised him against any covenants. He weighed the gravity of the occasion and chose to maintain silence.

The stream was diverted by Vichitravirya's entry. He had grown in years but not in health, Bhishma could gauge. He came in stumbling along as one in a drunken state.

He paid obeisance to Bhishma reluctantly, when pressed by his mother, who reminded Bhishma of his vow to abdicate the kingdom. "Therefore," she said, "it leaves Vichitravirya as the only heir to the Bharata dynasty. You may protect him or leave him helpless. He will be then killed by some enemy and that will be the end of this clan. As you wish."

Bhishma was visibly confounded.

"You had pledged, Devavrata," Satyavati said, "that when your father was dead, my son would inherit the throne of Hastinapur."

"Yes, mother. And I adhere to my pledge. Neither will Vichitravirya be helpless nor will the Bharata dynasty come to an end and nor will the kingdom of the Kurus be extinguished."

"Who will defend them?"

"I, your son Bhishma!"

"Promise?"

"I promise that Vichitravirya and his descendants will occupy the throne of Hastinapur and rule over the land of the Kurus for generations to come."

A glint of triumph flashed in Satyavati's eyes and the next moment it was replaced by innocent tears.

20

It was most shocking. Bhishma could not bring himself to believe what met his eyes. How could a Kuru prince behave in that manner? Drunk and surrounded by wenches without shame!

More so, the prince was impudently rude with Bhishma. "I am Vichitravirya, the future king of the Kurus. You may get beheaded at my command. Now go and don't try to act superior in my presence." Was it the same Vichitravirya who had only recently prostrated before him at the behest of his mother? Bhishma wondered. Still, he decided not to ignore the present state of debauchment and inebriation in which he had caught Vichitravirya, for that foreboded a fatal end for the teenager. He slapped the prince hard on his face.

"Is this how a crown prince ought to behave!" Bhishma roared. "You blemisher of the pride of the Kuru clan! You command your mentors to call you crown prince! Come, I will coronate you right now." And he dragged the lad upto Satyavati's chamber.

Satyavati was split in her mind about the event. The fact that Bhishma had slapped her son at once outraged her pride as the queen mother, who wanted to do the same to Bhishma who had dared to raise his hand against her son, "the future king of the Kurus." The other Satyavati wanted to bless Bhishma and say, "my son! Had you slapped Chitrangada instead, he wouldn't have been killed by the Gandharwa king." And perhaps, there was a third Satyavati who had chosen to keep quiet in the fear that this Bhishma who had raised his hand might raise a sword in the coming days, and cursed herself why she had invited him to Hastinapur.

Anyway her prime concern was to safeguard Vichitravirya now, not only against the enemies' sword but also against disease, affliction, and adventure of sensual kind.

As she spoke to Vichitravirya, she was curiously mellow. "You may go, my son!" she said. "Behave yourself and learn to respect your mentors. To the Kurus, insulting the mentors is an unpardonable sin."

Vichitravirya eyed her furtively. Was it the same mother who degraded Bhishma as her sworn enemy!

Satyavati commanded a complete privacy with Bhishma. "No one should be let in until my further orders," she told her maid. To Bhishma, she poured out her heart, her concerns about Vichitravirya, offering that it was her own fault. As Bhishma disagreed with her, she explained, "when your father wished to send these children to a sishikul (a school run by some sage), I opposed him. Chintrangada's pride and Vichitravirya's passion assumed alarming proportions, and I sat pretty and ignored that. I took it in a light vein as an essential feature of the kshatriyas. Their father was not there, and I lived amidst splendour and authority and, thus, ignored the import of abstinence and courtesy. Who could have disciplined them then? Of course, there were you, but you regarded them as strangers. Now when you have slapped him, I feel you have used your authority as his elder brother for once. I hope you will also fulfil your responsibility!"

It was decided between them that marriage was the only way out of this mire for Vichitravirya. But was Vichitravirya eligible for marriage, Bhishma contended.

"No! He is just fifteen," Satyavati said. She was

disheartened.

"Which is a time for his physical and mental development. We must put him under abstinence and discipline for at least ten years."

Satyavati doubted its feasibility in Vichitravirya's case. But Bhishma wished an attempt in that direction.

"Do try it," said Satyavati. "May you succeed in that! I wish you to take the responsibility of this younger brother of yours. It has been on my mind for long, only that I could not speak out. Even now, if you had not slapped him, I may not be able to express it. Take care of his education and discipline, and decide his marriage at a right time. Find him a match. Coronate him at an early hour of your choice. Help him stand up on his feet."

Bhishma was pleasantly surprised at Satyavati's transformation but assured her that he would take care of her son.

"If only your assuring words could convince me. But when I see Vichitravirya in that condition, it does not raise any hope forhis future. You and Vichitravirya are the two spontaneous channels of this stream of the Kuru dynasty. You I have blocked and, therefore, if this stream would not run forward through Vichitravirya, not only will this stream vanish but also the stigma will be on me, which I cannot endure."

Though Bhishma felt even more burdened in liability, his confidence was intact. "I have already told you not to worry. Not only Vichitravirya but many generations of his posterity will occupy the throne of Hastinapur and rule over this land of the Kurus."

"Let it be so, my son!" Satyavati sounded a bit relieved. Though soon after Bhishma's departure, her doubts returned to haunt her. Suppose he enthroned Vichitravirya and remained a regulator, he would be the virtual ruler!

A metaphor occurred to her in those moments. A pitcher was otherwise independent and capable. But if it had to be filled with water, a noose had to be tied round its neck and thrown into the well's depths. Then the same noose would pull it up and be discarded as superfluous after the water was obtained. The noose would lie on the ground and the pitcher would be placed on the water bearer's head. If she intended to fill the water of kingdom into Vichitravirya's pitcher, she must adorn the noose of Bhishma round her son's neck. Once the water was filled and the pitcher was able to hold it, the noose would lie on the ground and the pitcher would be placed on the water bearer's head.

A quaint image that! Anyway, Bhishma's arrival in Hastinapur had silenced the war cries of the Gandharvas, Panchals and Matsyas. Moreover, the everyday uprisings had also receded.

Notably, Bhishma had been observing the sanctity of his vow for eighteen years. He had never violated that. And he was past the age of aggressiveness.

'No, he won't betray me!' so mused Satyavati and lamented - only if she could believe all that.

Back at his place, Bhishma summoned the acharya and lost no time in coming to the point.

"What do you think about your disciple, acharya?" Bhishma hit the nail on the head.

The acharya was caught unawares. "I don't quite get what you mean," he said.

Bhishma smiled. "I just want to know about the overall progress of Vichitravirya who is your disciple and my younger brother. Acharya! He is the future ruler of this land. His parents have given him birth, but it is upto you to make him the king."

The acharya was peevish. He lamented that Vichitravirya was haughty and conceited and, therefore, did not regard him as his teacher. "He regards himself more as my provider than my disciple. The queen mother too did not let him be bound in discipline under me. Consequently, he even defied her. A boy first challenges his guardian's control and then his teacher's. Vichitravirya first went off the queen mother's hands, and much later mine."

"But this outcome does not please," said Bhishma.

"I know," the acharya endorsed him. "But where a guardian would not respect the teacher and the mentor, their child is sure to be in such a plight."

"Curse not, acharya, please!" Bhishma spoke low. "We have now to put the prince on to the right path, for which I need your support."

"It's already too late. Yet, we can try."

"Well then, we will make one fresh attempt," said Bhishma.

21

The rajavaidya (royal physician) checked Vichitravirya's pulse and sank into a long contemplation. He sat long in that state, his eyes closed.

Even as Bhishma waited in anticipation, Satyavati could not hold long and prodded the rajavaidya to speak out.

When granted his request for privacy, the royal physician said: "As I told you earlier, the prince has no stamina left to allow him to indulge in cohabitation. But you did not follow my advice. Medicines are effective only when acts that generate and proliferate a disease are stopped."

Satyavati bluntly denied any such lapse and insisted that the prince had been observing strict abstinence on her advice.

The physician refused to buy her argument. "Queen mother!" he said, "The prince has indulged in women and wine at a very young age in excessive measure. To be frank, if this practice is not put to a full stop, no physician in the world will be able to save him."

The physician's stand was vindicated by Vichitravirya's female attendant, who confessed that the prince had lately been seeing at least five new maids. The physician tried to console and convince Satyavati. "Queen mother," he said, "if the prince observes abstinence, my medicine can still do wonders."

Satyavati assured the royal physician of strict compliance of his instructions. Still she felt it was time to castigate herself. It was much of her own doing. It was she who taught her sons that indulgence, and not abstinence, was, in her viewhallmark of a royal person. If she was to teach abstinence to her sons even as King Shantanu's consort, what was the fun in submitting her youth to satisfy the lust of an old man. She criticized herself for her ignorance about distinguishing what was in her interest and what was not.

Alarmed by Satyavati's visible nervousness, Bhishma pleaded her not to worry too much.

"How not to worry, my son," her disconsolation was starkly exposed. "Vichitravirya is in an awful condition. Will he be saved?"

"Why not!" Bhishma's words had conviction. "The rajavaidya has categorically stated that if he practises abstinence, all is still not lost. And abstinence is not an impossible condition, mother."

"And that is one thing that was not taught to him. I regarded the royal indulgences as the bliss of life, not recognising that it was poison ... Chitrangada is gone and I fear the same for Vichitravirya. In that situation, my son, what fate is there for King Shantanu's dynasty?"

Bhishma was still optimistic when he said: "What is wrong with Vichitravirya? An excessive dose of wine and women. The abstinence will compensate the extra loss of energy. He will be well."

"May your words be true, my son!" said Satyavati. "But you will not marry. If I order Vichitravirya to live in abstinence, both of you brothers will remain childless. And if I permit him to be a householder, he will die of his ailment."

Bhishma was enlightened. For thefirst time, he felt her plea was not totally ignorable. If really the Bharata dynasty could have no heir left! Then?

Bhishma realised he had left Satyavati far behind in the mind game of concocting the worst. A physician is wont to assuring the patient. No physician would ever say that there were no chances of survival for his patient. If Vichitravirya was virtually on the verge of death, what was his future? A life of abstinence in which there was no marriage, no wife, no child? And who could assure that after recuperation Vichitravirya would still practise abstinence. Or else the Nature would allow him a sufficient lease of life till recuperation to practise abstinence?

'Will the onus be back on me to produce an heir to the Bharata dynasty?' Bhishma mused and flinched at the idea of violating his own pledge.

And, if in a contingency, as in the event of Vichitravirya's demise even before his marriage, will they condemn Bhishma for stalling the matrimony of the ailing and sick Vichitravirya so that he would pass away without producing an heir to the Kuru dynasty and Bhishma would regain the kingdom of Hastinapur? If that happened, Bhishma would not be able to live with that calumny.

He recalled, and readily recommended marriage as anideal resort for Vichitravirya. Satyavatithough differed, saying that the rajavaidya had advised him to avoid woman's company.

"Carnal indulgence is not making him sick, mother," Bhishma observed. "The disproportionate measure of carnal indulgence is his sickness.Human society has devised marriage to moderate the indulgence in carnal activities."

"However, Vichitravirya has still not reached the marriageable age."

"He hasn't even reached an age when he should indulge in adventures of sensual kind either or drink," Bhishma argued.

Satyavati should have realised it much earlier, she mused. If so, she would not have lost Chitrangada in the first place or have Vichitravirya pushed into the present crisis. The king was right in his remark that the birds would not allow their chicks to leave the nest before they had grown wings and the kshatriya kings would not let their sons enter a royal palace until they had completed the stage of celibacy. A potter makes a pot with raw mud and puts it in an oven to be baked; not a drop of water would he allow to fall upon it until it is baked and then even neck-deep immersion would do it no harm. The schools run by the sages (the rishikulas) are the kilns where princes are seasoned. After they are out of it, no amount of carnal pleasures can corrupt them.

Thus did Satyavati think and relented at least to urge Bhishma to "find some suitable princess, who should be religious and not passionate."

Back in her chamber she felt exhausted and ordered privacy so that she could relax.

Even as she tried to sleep, an islet emerged before her closed eyes, and she saw there in an ashram Krishna Dvaipayana, who was no more a child but a youth past celibate. She could not deduce whether he had assumed a householder's life or not.

At once, Krishna Dvaipayana's matted hair was undone and beard disappeared. Silk replaced his bark attire. His eyes opened and the deep dullness of spiritualism in them gave way to a gay warmth. Satyavati decked him, who had meanwhile got up and sat upon the throne, with various ornaments and lastly crowned him.

The bards shouted, 'Hail Krishna Dvaipayana, the universal king of Hastinapur.' Satyavati looked up sky wards and wished if that could be true.

22

The emissaries dispatched by Bhishma to various kingdoms to find a girl for Vichitravirya returned with messages that were mostly not only disappointing but utterly insulting. Some of those royal families took recourse to the fact that Vichitravirya was not mature enough to marry. Others were too blunt to hide their disgust for him and his demeanour. Some even went to the extent of questioning the honour of the Kuru dynasty which, they insisted, had been rendered vulnerable and shaky following the old king's demise, whereas the kshatriya prince had renounced and now that feeble, sick and impotent Vichitravirya, who had a mean Nishada mother's blood in his veins, was going to be enthroned... who would marry off his daughter to such a one ... Some of them even predicted Vichitravirya's untimely death in immediate future or, they suggested, he would be strangled by a maid or slaughtered by some mighty ruler as the Gandhavaraja had killed Chitrangada, and there would be no Kuru kingdom and no Kuru clan left on this earth.

Eventually, a messenger arrived with an encouraging news about the king of Kashi who had three daughters-Amba, Ambika and Ambalika-of which Ambalika the youngest one was a little older than Vichitravirya.

Was Kashiraja willing to marry Ambalika to Vichitravirya, Bhishma demanded and was informed that the king of Kashi had proposed a swayamvara (in which a girl chooses a husband for herself) and would like Vichitravirya to participate. The decision was to be taken by the girls, and honoured by their father.

Bhishma concluded that the Kashiraja had neither rejected nor accepted his proposal explicitly and there was no reason to blame him for that. Swayamvara was then not only in vogue among the Kshatriyas but also highly honoured as a custom of marriage. Several royal families even retained the age-old tradition where they demanded a certain amount of money in lieu of their daughter, though it was no longer considered graceful by the Aryavarta kings, just as they despised illegitimate sons and polyandry. The society was passing through a transitional phase, Bhishma thought on. Giving off a girl against a certain amount of money was a diabolic patriarchal trend which awarded no rights to women, who could be bartered like an animal or object by their father or brother. So was the custom of a son born of an unwed woman a remnant of the same society, which treated women as a means of production, and solicited them to deliver as many children as they could immediately after they attained puberty.On the other hand, polyandry was a remnant of matriarchal society where a woman was supreme.

Back to the question of Vichitravirya's marriage, Bhishma was in no uncertain mind that the king of Kashi had in no way been contemptuous to the Kurus. He knew Vichitravirya would not be acceptable to any of his daughters. He knew Vichitravirya was too frail to even travel up to Kashi.

What could Bhishma do in such a situation? Kashiraja, like any other king of the time, had called for a swayamvara that was gaining currency by the day. And obviously, there seemed the scantiest chances of Vichitravirya qualifying the contest.

But Bhishma was determined that he would not under any circumstance subscribe to a suggestion that 'just about any girl will do.' Vichitravirya had already been carrying the stigma of being a lowly woman's son, and Bhishma would not let it pass on to his posterity. Vichitravirya's wife must be the daughter of a ruling king so that the future generations of the rulers of Hastinapur would not be looked down upon by the Kshatriyas.

Satyavati was reasonably concerned about her son's matrimony and constantly pestered Bhishma on that account. Bhishma's concern was to stay clear of any suspicions. He would never relish to let anyone conclude that he did not want Vichitravirya to have an heir so that he could regain the kingdom of Hastinapur. He did not want any such accusation made against him.

He got nostalgic about his cottage across the Ganga where he had been enjoying his freedom from the turmoil of the kingdom and the ostentatious authority and all else that came with it. But even in his present freedom he was not liberated from the affairs of the state. Though not a king himself, he was responsible for a safe and capable line of rulers of Hastinapur. He must fulfil his promise made to mother Satyavati.

To achieve that, Bhishma would do whatever was essential, even despite himself. If preparations were on for the swayamvara of the three princesses of Kashi, he resolved that he would win them for Vichitravirya by hook or by crook. He was not going to entertain any pleas against that. What if Vichitravirya lacked guts to win a consort for himself through a swayamvara, Bhishma would honour his pledge by any means, fair or foul.

Abduction was anoption. Bhishma could try even that if it became inevitable. A girl was anyway a giftable item. What if her father, the Kashiraja, would not gift her, Bhishma would win and then gift her away.

23

Bhishma ordered his charioteer to halt the carriage at a spot far away from the main town. He knew his charioteer felt it queer to stop at such an unlikely place. But he himself had no explanations to offer. In fact, he was still not sure about his specific intention. However, he was firm that he had to fetch a wife for Vichitravirya from there against any odds.

He was sorely hurt that the king of Kashi had not extended a formal invitation to him or the kingdom of Hastinapur for the swayamvara. And that was one reason why he was there. He must settle his score. He had to punish the king for his impudence.

He spotted a cluster of trees beside the Ganga and decided to camp there, enthused by the fact that the tree formed a soothing shade and allowed certain privacy to any wayfarer. Besides, it suited his purpose as he did not wish any unsolicited glances or curiosity from any passer by and the place being singularly secluded promised to shield against any such probability. Though he had to tackle his charioteer Virsen's prying on that account.

"Virsen! We are not invited," Bhisma tried to explain. "We are here of our own will. For that simple reason, we will not avail of the Kashiraja's hospitality."

Virsen was least interested. He only noted that Bhishma had not brought any soldiers with him. There were two other chariots, which had a few attendants and enough arms on them.

The swayamvara pavilion was erected in a vast ground within the city ramparts adjoining the banks of the Ganga. The invited kings were accommodated in the camps close by, whereas the soldiers and the servants were staying further away.

Bhishma found the site scantily crowded when he stepped in. A few kings present there were apparently engaged in formal introductions, which did not interest Bhishma who had never been 'sociable' that way. He felt it more delectable watching those pack of characters in myriad colours and countenances. The youths among them had evidently taken him as one of the suitors and seemed amply amused.

A middle-aged man was in striking contrast to Bhishmain that he had his hair coloured to feign youth, which aroused repugnance in Bhishma who found it fairly funny. Will the black hair make this man young, he mused. Will the blackness of hair conceal the wrinkles on his face? And even if the wrinkles were concealed, will his youth be reversed? What was important - to be young or to look young? And why should he crave for youth? To remarry? To bluff a princess? To remain arrested by passion? If passion was releasing him, why should he, instead of recognising his release, be trying to detain it with his greedy paws? He had not only coloured his hair but also used other toiletries; it seemed he had bathed not with the Ganga water but taken dips in a pool of perfumes.

When Bhishma presented himself at the initial round of introduction, obviously he attracted hostile glances and comments from a section of the contestants. Though suppressed, the remarks were loud enough to be heard by Bhishma.

"We were told Bhishma had renounced."

"I am not aware of that. But yes, I was told he had vowed to observe celibacy throughout."

"He vowed to observe celibacy, not to refrain from joining a swayamvara."

"Anyway, no one is eager here to select him. The poor man sits here all by himself. And if he soothes his eyes by watching the princesses, what is wrong in that?"

"But he had even abdicated his kingdom, hadn't he?"

"Yes."

"Who let him into this swayamvara of princesses then?"

Bhishma tried to avoid all that in spite of himself. Otherwise...

He did not want to react clumsily at this juncture.

Meanwhile, the king of Kashi was at the assembly introducing his three daughters.

"My eldest daughter Amba," the king announced.

Bhishma looked at her. She was beautiful, exceptionally beautiful! She was around twenty-eight. A mature age, Bhishma decided, for a girl offering herself at a swayamvara. Otherwise, immature girls were not able to pick a suitable mate for themselves due to lack of worldly wisdom that comes with a matured age. That was perhaps why her father had not pressed for marriage so far, which was practically uncommon among the royal families. Anyway, Vichitravirya, at hardly seventeen, was no match for her.

Bhishma challenged his own judgement about Amba's beauty. What was beautiful about her, he questioned himself.

'There is nothing so beautiful in her,' an inner voice protested. 'All the charm lies in youth. Nature has designed man likethat. It has put iron particles in woman's form and man's eyes have been endowed with traits of a magnet! The attraction lies not in a woman's beauty, but weakness is embedded in man's heart. You have not only vowed to remain unmarried but to observe strict celibacy. Whatever we designate as happiness is but an illusory mask of grief.

You must recognise the face behind the mask. You have resolved to break the bonds of Nature, to transcend your limits. If you wish to be liberated from the illusion of Nature, you must recognise the stakes Nature has pitched within you to keep you enslaved.'

"This is my second daughter Ambika," declared the Kashiraja with aplomb.

Bhishma was jolted back from his wanton reverie. He looked up: Ambika was around seven years younger than Amba. Though not suitable age-wise to be Vichitravirya's wife, the difference would be comparatively less. She was delicate and stood there fazed and befuddled, perhaps raring to run away at the shortest hint.

At last, there was "my third daughter Ambalika." She was around five years younger than Ambika, virtually a charming teen. A couple of years older than Vichitravirya, she was still closest to him among the three of them.

The round of introduction commenced and the girls went round surveying the contenders.

When they approached Bhishma, he stood up and solemnly declared that Devavrata Bhishma was not here as a suitor. And defying the raised brows and uncertain questions lurking in the eyes of those present, including the princesses, he proclaimed: "Kashiraja, the royal family of Kashi and all the kings present here, let all of you listen. I am in the presence of this kshatriya congregation for abducting these princesses of Kashi. You are all brave, well-armed warriors, you are free to engage with me and stall me. You may even kill me and retrieve the princesses. If I am killed, the princesses could lawfully select a groom for themselves; and if you are vanquished, I will according to the kshatriya tradition take them to Hastinapur."

He lifted his huge bow and commanded the princesses: "Come out of the pavilion. My chariot waits there."

The Kashiraja had never anticipated such a contingency. He was caught unawares, not knowing what to do if at all he was in a position to do something. He looked at the kings who were there to contest the swayamvara. They all stood there, more as beaus than warriors.

Bhishma repeated his challenge. "Princesses!" he addressed the three girls. "Don't compel me to use force. Go and take your seats in the chariot. In the meanwhile, this assembly of kings may decide whether to fight or not."

As they walked away toward the carriage led by Amba, even Bhishma was amazed that the bunch of suitors offered no resistance. Rather, they made way for them.

The Kashiraja admonished the kings for their cowardice and tried to urge them to take on Bhishma.

Sobhraj Shalva was one among them who took the challenge. "Bhishma! Wait," he shouted. "I will not let you go as that. Wait! Let me put on my armour."

Bhishma smiled, "Shalva! I am here. Why you alone, tell all these kings that they may prepare for fight; put on their armours; acquire arms, and call for their carriages and drivers. I am not a bandit who will catch you unawares and elope with the princesses at once. I am a kshatriya of the Bharata clan. I have put up my challenge. Now I allow you time for preparation, even an opportunity to fight. If I take away these girls without any combat, I will be undermining their worth. I would never like to be accused of abducting the girls for whom no prince was willing to fight."

Bhishma was confident. He had enough arms and skill to use them. He had been trained by great gurus and his faithful assistants were with him. He stood flashing a nonchalant smile even as Amba watched the unparalleled warrior in him.

The fight was ignited by Shalva who shot the first arrow. He was joined by several other kings. Amba was stunned to watch Bhishma alone out-manoeuvring them all. The rival kings were indiscriminate in their use of arms whereas Bhishma was most calculative and therefore successful and victorious.

Shortly, it was evident that even the combined force of all those kings was no match for Bhishma as a warrior. Mostkings were exhausted except Shalva who was still shooting arrows with undaunted zeal.

"O kshatriya!" Bhishma exclaimed. "I appreciate your zeal and heartily regard your courage. But I am here to fetch the girls and not kill the helpless. If this battle is stretched any further, your lieutenants will forsake the ground and it will be the end of you. So I now drive off my carriage. Stop it if you can."

Bhishma signalled to his charioteer. His chariot took a round of the battlefield and took the turn leading out of the town. There was no resistance, except for Shalva who chased and challenged Bhishma, "Stop! You cannot flee the field unless you have defeated me."

"You may fulfil your wish to fight. Bhishma would not even imagine to flee the field."

And Bhishma accelerated his volley of arrows. Ambika closed her eyes in fright. Ambalika looked the other way, and Amba's eyes roved between Shalva and Bhishma, as if to judge the better of them.

Shalva was severely wounded and his chariot was the first to bite dust. The two horses were killed by Bhishma and the carriage came to a halt.

Bhishma confronted Shalva who lay on the ground exposed to Bhishma's sword. But Bhishma spared him: "I do not kill the defenceless, not even for a swayamvara. My mission is attained. Say not Bhishma has fled the field."

He sheathed back his sword, mounted his carriage, and commanded: "Let's go, charioteer!"

24

Kashi was left far behind. Yet, much to Amba's surprise, Bhishma was still alert. Did he anticipate an onslaught from her father, the king? The thought amused her and she almost laughed. She looked at her two sisters, who sat huddled together like frightened birds. Why should they fear, she wondered. At the swayamvara, they had anyway presented themselves for marriage and their marriage would still happen; the only difference was that at the swayamvara in Kashi there were a number of princes and kings and they could select any one of them and now they had no option. Bhishma's will was their fate, their future. Even their father was unlikely to object; marriage was on his mind, and marry they would. Had he chosen a match for them, the consequence would have been his responsibility. He would have then gone by the custom in vogue and charged a fee for them, which might have made him an object of slander. Now, many royal families were awakened to the contrast between a bride's sale and her marriage which was an honourable custom that established relations with a new family, where the father of the bride paid a certain dowry whose amount decided her respect in the new household. As she would be the mistress in her new home, her father's side was also deemed to make a convincing contribution. Or, it might have been calculated that a man's property was inherited by his sons and, therefore, he gave out her share at the time of her departure from his house.

Now, as the events had unfolded, their father was exempted from any expenses, nor had he to face any slur on that account. They had been abducted to be a part of the celebrated kshatriya clan of Hastinapur.

Was it why their father had been deferring their marriage? Was he waiting for such a thing to happen? Why did he not care for at least Amba and Ambika who had come of age? Was he too busy to think of that, or was he devoid of all pragmatism, or was he oblivious of his daughters, or for some reason did not wish to marry them off?

Amba recalled, when she was sixteen - and Ambika ten and Ambalika five - her mother had urged him to find a match for her, and he had tried to make excuses. Her mother had insisted that a father must assume responsibility, whether he was a commoner or a king. A queen could not excuse herself from delivering a child simply because she was a queen. She would give birth to a child like an ordinary woman and rear it.

The same scene was enacted on Ambika's sixteenth birthday and then on Ambalika's attaining the same age. Their mother was so outraged in frustration that she declared, "If you don't marry off your daughters they would, instead of producing babies as wives, do it as our daughters. Will you accept their illegitimate children?"

"The sages regard illegitimate children equally sacred and respectable," her father had sounded unconcerned in his remark.

"But the kshatriya community do not accept such children now. They have come to consider it a stigma."

Her father brushed it off with a shrug. "Let them do if they want," he seemed to suggest.

Gradually her mother was increasingly becoming insistent and father apathetic. Eventually, she had to pay for her insistence. She got bedridden. The more insistent she grew, the more indisposed she became.

Then, one fine day Shalva, the king of Sobha, came to see her father. The way he looked at Amba stirred her deep within.

"O Princess! You are so beautiful, so exceptionally beautiful. Wonder if you are Urvashi," he remarked and before her embarrassment could slip into denial, he was straight forward:

"Princess! I want to marry you; will you be my wife?"

"My father will not approve of it."

"Why?

Why?" Shalva demanded again.

"Can't say. But I feel so."

"Ambe!" Shalva addressed her by her name, "I am the ruling king of Sobha. How could the Kashiraja reject me?"

"It is not that he will reject you. It is simply that he is in no mood to marry me off."

"If you are not formally married to me, I will abduct you. Though not willingly, I will even fight with your father if required. I will win through a river of blood,tread over a thousand corpses in the battlefield, and take you away."

Ambika found him even more irrepressible. She loved his talks as if he was not talking about war and bloodshed, but about the flowers blossoming in spring.

"I cannot live without you, O Princess!"

These were the sweetest words Amba had ever been subjected to.

The Kashiraja, however, raised no questions with Shalva. He acquiesced at the very drop of the proposal. Shalva could take her away any moment he desired. Even right then.

Her mother, though, put a spanner this time. She intervened saying that princesses were not married off in that manner. There had to be celebrations and a throng of invitees on the occasion. It was a question of a king's status after all. Then there were Ambika and Ambalika. What about them? Would he wait for another Shalva to come asking for their hand?

"What do you mean to say, pray? Crack no riddles," the Kashiraja said.

"Plan a swayamvara like a kshatriya king. Invite kings from every corner of Jambudweepa. Let Amba take Shalva, and let Ambika and Ambalika too select a groom. I will marry them off and be redeemed of my liability at once. I just cannot afford to put in as many years of painful wait as I did in Amba's case."

Her father consented readily, leaving Amba wondering that if her father had no reservations about the swayamvara, why did he not arrange it earlier! What was the problem?

The problem was revealed when Bhishma rose to announce his intent. He literally drove the three sisters to his chariot.

Shalva, though, put in the best of his might. He fought so heroically, Amba loved his every move and was flattered that it was all for her sake. A woman recognises her worth when a man puts his life at stake for her. She had so far never realised that she was so important that a man should fight for her, shed his blood for her or kill another man.

Amba was enchanted while Shalva faced defeat. When his horses were slain and his charioteer lay groaning on the field, she looked at Shalva, who was all the more spectacular in his impotent rage. And then, perhaps for the first time, she eyed the victor Bhishma, who looked like a recluse in a royal attire. He wore no ornaments, neither was not proud of his victory. Still, there was something definitely alarming in that strong man. He had a few gray hair on his head and beard, but he was not so old. His rough and tough look was certainly charming.

25

Beside the Ganga near Prayag, a brief halt was taken at Bhishma's behest. Ambika and Ambalika looked scared of Bhishma whereas Amba was amused. Her hesitant smile distracted Bhishma for once.

"We will relax here for a while," he said. "You may wash if you so wish. The Ganga will take away your fatigue."

"We know. Ganga is our mother," blurted Amba.

Bhishma was taken aback: Ganga was his mother. Who called Ganga her mother! He looked back and saw Amba. "How?" he quizzed her.

"We are from Kashi," she was frank in her speech. "We regard the Ganga as our mother."

Bhishma's lips curved in a gentle smiled and agreed with her. He asked them to partake of some refreshments.

And, as an afterthought, he turned to Amba. "Ambe! Tell your sisters there is no reason to be scared or uncomfortable. Convince them that they are safe. The Kurus honour women."

By the time they reached Hastinapur after a couple of more halts, Amba found Bhishma gradually relaxing. He was now more of their guardian than abductor. She and her sisters were his honourable guests whose comfort was his duty.

At the city gate, they were extended a grand reception. Amba still wondered why Bhishma had not taken armed men along if he had abduction on his mind. Did this man think he could engage single-handed with the entire pack of the Aryavarta kings and even vanquish them? Was he so dauntless and daring? She wished she could hold his hand, look straight into his eyes, smile and urge him not to be so adventurous again. She blushed at the thought.

At the palace, the three girls were welcomed by the Mother Queen Satyavati, who was delighted and admired their pristine charm. She ordered her maid to make arrangements for their rest. Amba was the last of the three to retire, though reluctantly and only after she was commanded by Bhishma.

Then Satyavati turned to Bhishma. "The princesses are beautiful but why all the three? Ambalika would have done for our Vichitravirya."

Bhishma resorted to his wit as he said, "One queen is never sufficient for a king, mother! Although Vichitravirya is an excellent appraiser of the feminine.... It may not be feasible for me to travel frequently to fetch a queen for the king every time. So I brought as many as I could manage in one go."

The Queen Mother laughed at his funny remark but was still wary of the age-difference between Vichitravirya and Amba, and even her two sisters. Bhishma reminded her of the haste he had to make at the swayamvara which ruled out any selection.

Back in his chamber, Bhishma was haunted by the Queen Mother's remark. Did she question his intention behind bringing all the three sisters? Did he... If the three of them were married to Vichitravirya, Amba, being senior, might not appeal to Vichitravirya as intensely as the other two. He might not like Amba at all. If an abducted princess was neglected by her husband, what would be livable in her life? What about Amba's fate? Bhishma had once proudly announced that he did not kill the vulnerable. But what about that? Was that not killing someone vulnerable? If Amba was forced to live the rest of her life as a neglected forsaken woman, won't she be cursing Bhishma all her life? Which was even more painful than slaying.

Better to marry Ambika and Ambalika to Vichitravirya. But Amba? What about her? Should she be wed to Bhishma? He thought inside his mind a villain was laughing at his plight.

Bhishma tried his utmost to shoo away that villain but he was too resolute. The ensuing debate focussed around Bhishma's avowed celibacy.

"Were you not aroused with desire the moment you saw Amba? Be honest," challenged the villain.

"I am willing to break the bonds but I have never claimed to have done that. If it were so easy, everyone would have severed the bonds of delusion and ignorance. We are stuck in a peculiar state. The individual in us stands neck deep in the pond of delusion. Till the awareness exists, an individual labours to keep off the water. The moment the awareness is loosened, he slips and is drowned in that water, which proves fatal for him," Bhishma conceded.

"That's why," the villain contended, "when there is no emancipation, why do you strive to push away that surge of water? You know drowning is your fate, so all such effort is futile. Stop resisting the water. Enjoy its cool feel. Sport in it. Swim, bathe, splash, have a dip, and then you will see how it thrills your body and mind."

Bhishma still protested saying: "Drowning may be the fate but the strategy has to be struggle."

"In the face of an inevitable defeat, what use is struggle?"

"To a kshatriya, even being killed is a gain."

The villain wanted to say that the Kshatriyas were fools but instead he said, "You took vows to be liberated from bonds but are you free? Don't you feel an ordinary householder, though tied to his household, enjoys both the stability and smoothness of that bond! And you are an idiot sweating out on somebody else's field, where you own neither the ground nor the produce! This is the time you realized it. If you want to do farming, go to your fields. If you aspire to foster a people, let it be your own people. If you want to run a household, let it be your own household."

That was enough to enrage Bhishma whose eyes became moist. He felt shattered because the villain was a part of himself. He had so far assumed that he had washed away his defilements, that his mind was liberated from all illusion, all fear, all malice, all feelings of yours and mine. But no, in fact, he was no different from an ordinary individual on that account. In his mind also was the same filth and darkness that eroded the soil from under a man's feet and drifted him away.

Finally Bhishma sought solace in the rushing stream of the Ganga, who had been and still was a mother to him, soothing and comforting him in such moments of melancholy.

26

Vichitravirya was enthroned in a grand ceremony amidst great pomp and show. It was a happier occasion for Satyavati than Chitrangada's coronation. In fact, Chitrangada had met his end even before he could be married. But Vichitravirya was secure in that he was not inclined to war. He would neither go a-hunting nor for a duel. Also Chitrangada could not enjoy Bhishma's support for Bhishma was not at Hastinapur in those days. Vichitravirya was absolutely under Bhishma's protection and Bhishma was committed to defending him. Satyavati had heard about Bhishma's military exploits but acknowledged his prowess only after his recent act of valour while abducting the three Kashi sisters, as related to her by Bhishma's charioteer Virsen.

Though not admitting Virsen's account as absolute truth, Satyavati could still not ignore that Bhishma had abducted the three girls from their swayamvara, where the whole pack of the Aryavarta kings was camping for the same purpose. Obviously, they would have fought with him. And supposing there had been no combat, one could not conclude that they behaved so out of their love for Bhishma; the more plausible reason was that they dared not. If Chitrangada had resorted to Bhishma's might instead of his own, he would have been spared the fate he met. Had Bhishma vanquished the Gandharva king, a vast chunk of his land could be annexed. And had Bhishma been killed by the Gandharva king, there would be no need to go to war and Chitrangada could strike a truce with him. However, in the absence of Chitrangada, Vichitravirya must exploit Chitrangada's experiences. He must also exploit Bhishma's gallant acumen. Let Bhishma's arms defend the empire and Vichitravirya enjoy its fruits. Let the subjects be fostered by Bhishma and Vichitravirya be their master. Let Bhishma be made a nurse who would have all the liabilities of a mother but no rights.

Did she have no love, no soft corner for Bhishma? Satyavati asked herself. But instantly she poured a bucket of water on that spark. She had even loved Parashar once.

That reminded her of Krishna Dvaipayana who, she had heard, had grown up into a sage now, venerable like his father. But her inhibition was such that she could not invite him even to Vichitravirya's coronation, not even as the sacrificing priest performing the yajna.

The coronation ceremony was immediately followed by the preparations for his marriage. If given the liberty, Satyavati would have solemnised Vichitravirya's nuptial vows right after his enthronement. But the wisdom of Bhishma and the ministers prevailed, who suggested that a king's wedding had to be a formal ceremonial affair.

Satyavati had no one to confide to how eager she was to get her son married. In fact, Chitrangada's untimely demise had thrown her off balance. She had that fear of a mishap embedded within her. Nevertheless, she wielded patience. Meanwhile, the various preparations continued.

Amba observed and heard a lot from her chambermaids, some informed her, others dropped hints for her in their conversation. A lot had been happening in Hastinapur since she had arrived there. First she was told about Vichitravirya's enthronement, which least interested or thrilled her. Anyway, her wish had not been honoured even in her own Kashi, and this was Hastinapur!

Her turn to be alarmed came when the chambermaid measured her wrist for bracelets and announced: "You will look more gorgeous than any nymph as a queen."

"Queen!" Amba exclaimed." But it is Queen Mother Satyavati's son, Vichitravirya, who had been installed as the king?"

"Of course! Why? It is his queen you are going to be," the chambermaid smiled.

"But we were abducted by Prince Bhishma..."

"Yes. He did it for our king who does not like wars. The elder prince deals with all such things," said the chambermaid. There was an enigmatic smile on her face.

Amba did not react. The chambermaid left.

Amba wished to see Bhishma, who presented himself without delay.

"You called me, Ambe?"

"You seem to be quite busy?"

"Everyone in Hastinapur is busy these days... making preparations for your wedding."

"My wedding or your king's?" said Amba sarcastically.

"What do you mean?" Bhishma looked up quizzed.

"Nothing in particular. I just wondered."

"But a wedding has to be both the bridegroom's and the bride's."

"So the groom is King Vichitravirya and the brides-we three sisters?"

"Yes. Why?"

"Why did you go there then to abduct us?"

Her query was devoid of any honorific. She was blunt and harsh. It was more of an accusation.

"Vichitravirya lacked courage to abduct you three. I did it on his behalf."

"You should have declared that at the pavilion in Kashi," Amba blurted out.

Bhishma looked on stunned. He recalled he had not

cared to mention it. But it was the abductor's privilege to give the abducted girls in marriage to whosoever he chose to.

"But it was overtly declared at the swayamvara while introducing me that I had vowed celibacy."

"I was peeved by that declaration that you had decided and announced to abduct us," she was trying to be more and more straightforward.

Bhishma discerned her mind but was restricted by his vow. He confessed, "Maybe it was my fault. I should have made the declaration. I committed that error."

"Then, O senior-most prince! I committed an error too. I could not tell you then that I had already accepted King Shalva of Sobha as my husband by my will and my father's consent. Had you not abducted me, I would have selected him at the swayamvara. Now you may do what you will."

Deep in anguish, Bhishma wanted to ask Amba: "When Shalva was engaged with me and when he staked his life, why did you keep quiet? Why did you not speak then? I would have released you that very moment and handed you over to Shalva. Had you opened your mouth then I would have understood why Shalva was so bent upon sacrificing his life. Why only he was aggressive and campaigned against me." But Bhishma refrained from any such outburst. Amba had returned his pleas back upon him.

"I feel that in such a circumstance, you should not be married to Vichitravirya. But I must first ask Mother Satyavati and the learned brahmins."

"If they do not agree with you, will I be married to Vichitravirya against my will? Will you succumb to others' will, your vow ignored?"

"No. No one has the right to violate my vow."

"Then, O great prince, you should honour my vow too and help me keep it."

"I will try," said Bhishma in utter desperation. He was outsmarted by Amba's cool and calculated pleas.

The learned brahmins, who were in Hastinapur to perform the nuptial rites, took a brief minute to decide. Their verdict was clear. A girl, who had secretly selected a certain man as her spouse, was virtually wedded to him and, therefore, could not be ethically married to another man. Even otherwise, if Amba was not married to Vichitravirya, he still would have two wives that were sufficient for him.

The state physician's advice, though not solicited, seconded the one-queen proposition. In his opinion it was not good for the king's well-being to have more than one wife. He advised Bhishma to marry the second princess too, which would leave the youngest one for Vichitravirya, though even one queen would potentially be risky for him.

With those views in mind, Bhishma approached Satyavati who at once was disconcerted. She called for Bhishma's opinion. He replied that he would go with the brahmins' view.

"Which implies...?"

"That Amba should not be married to Vichitravirya."

"But you abducted her for that purpose."

"Yes. But then I was not aware of her alliance with Shalva."

"If that was the case, she must have spoken out. She should have told you so when she was being abducted. The journey from Kashi to Hastinapur was long one; she had enough time at her hand. Here she has been mute as a rock all the way. Now when the preparations for her marriage are accomplished, her love for Shalva is suddenly revived. She is playing with the honour of the royal family of Hastinapur," Satyavati said.

Bhishma wondered how a woman could be so apathetic to the feelings of another woman.

She proposed, "Give her another chance to think over it."

"Against her will?"

"The abducted princesses have no wish of their own."

Bhishma's silence prodded her to demand, "Anything

else?"

"Yes, our physician suggests that the king should not have more than one queen."

"So? Then let Amba go... Ask some maid to tell her she may go anywhere she likes."

"Yes, Mother Queen! I will do that."

Bhishma broke the news with a feigned nonchalance.

The subsequent uneasy silence was finally broken by Amba. "You are heartless, Bhishma!" she exploded. "You address me as 'Amba' even at this moment of expulsion."

The words created a turmoil in Bhishma's heart as would all the winds combined on the sea. But exhibiting that turmoil would be graceless and enfeeble Bhishma's vow. He could not suppress it. But it could certainly be ignored - an art which he had perfected by now. He had mostly ignored his feelings.

"My charioteer, Virsen, will drive you to King Shalva of Sobha. But for the king's wedding at Hastinapur, I would have taken you personally to Sobha and handed you over to your lover, just as I had brought you here."

Amba was outraged: "Whether burnt by the precious and pious wood or by the ordinary one, it makes no difference to the corpse."

"Princess, the hurt we get on our heart from the cremation, the sandalwood puts a cooling touch to that."

"I am soothed! That would suffice," Amba sounded subdued.

"One more favour. Don't leave the carriage anywhere until the destination is reached. When Virsen will be back with a message from Shalva, only then will I be contented."

"Your contentment will be my gain," said Amba with tears in her eyes.

Amba's imminent departure inspired fear in Ambalika while Ambika closed her eyes to conceal her surging emotions. Amba consoled her sisters, arguing that they were no more the abducted ones there but were going to be married to the king. Moreover, the two would be together there and, it was she who would be leaving alone.

"And remember," Amba's voice dropped to a whisper, "your greatest well-wisher here is your abductor Bhishma. You must approach him in any emergency."

That was all. Amba took their leave and climbed the chariot waiting for her. Virsen was alone. No sign of Bhishma. As informed by the charioteer, Bhishma was away on some urgent business.

Amba was confounded. Will she be happy with Shalva? Will he be happy with her? It must come as a celebration for Shalva who was going to have her, all thanks to Bhishma.

If Bhishma had not crossed her path, she would have garlanded Shalva as her chosen one. As a couple, they would enjoy a lovers' life all through. But what game Providence had played? Now she was to live with a stigma. Suppose anything unwarranted got exposed, what problems she would face in her conjugal life!

Amba was sunk in speculation.

The gateway of Hastinapur came.

Amba returned to her conscious self. She looked around. Lo! Bhishma sat there in his chariot, Virsen halted there.

"Princess! I had brought you to Hastinapur and, therefore, it is my duty to send you off," Bhishma spoke low. "I decided my absence at this juncture would amount to insolence."

"Thank you, Bhishma. May I beg another parting favour?"

"What's that?"

"You will look after my sisters like a guardian," Amba pleaded. "They are ignorant, stopping just short of being foolish. Keep them off all trouble."

"I will remember your words," Bhishma promised

and made way for her carriage.

Ambika and Ambalika were married to Vichitravirya in a grand pompous ceremony. Bhishma sweated it out as the father of the groom and the brides. His strenuous indulgence prompted quite a few of those around and Satyavati herself to admonish him not to overexert himself and to be discreet with his health.

Bhishma, in the depth of heart, knew that he was contesting against himself. The image of the parting Amba was so indelibly imprinted in his heart that all exercise to erase it proved futile. When solitary, he was concerned by that image. "You have done me wrong, Bhishma. I was indeed attracted to Shalva for there was no one in my life till then. But when you came up, I had to examine myself. You abducted me and I lost my heart to your valour. Of course, Shalva had also exhibited his gallantry but you did it all alone. Compared with Shalva, you stood up unmatched. You stirred amorous expectations in me when

you addressed me as 'Ambe' on our journey to Hastinapur. But your one sentence 'I had abducted you three to be married to Vichitravirya' hurled me from the highest pinnacle of the Himalayas down to the fathomless abyss of the sea," she seemed to say.

Though he realised that Amba's voice in his mind was his illusion, he was unable to silence it. All his suppressed desires were returning in the form of Amba. In fact, he had never been able to kill his desires.

His father had named him Bhishma after his stern vow. All the world knew no one could equal Bhishma in his resolve. Bhishma laughed at the idea. He knew how resolute he was and what Amba had done to it. He could not resist temptations. What he appeared to people and what he himself was were two different people.

Bhishma felt he was now fearing himself.

27

Vichitravirya woke up to a slight fever. He felt very weak in the body and his head felt heavy - which was not new to him after all those years. When he felt better and his frame was supportive, he would call the maids. When he found himself indisposed and a dullness visited his mind, he drank up a considerable amount of wine to obviate it. Just as he was coming to terms with that routine, Bhishma and his mother struck an accord, and he was given to spend his time more in the company of holy men than with the maids and wine. He had to drink the bitter potions prepared by the state physician. To aggravate that, his mother had colluded with Bhishma and made him the king. He was not averse to kingship but to the idea of attending the court everyday and considering the representations made by the ministers, the brahmins and others, which was virtually beyond him. He was more at home alone with a pitcher of wine.

As he opened his eyes, he found Ambika and Ambalika standing there, insisting that he visit the assembly, which awaited him as usual. He tried to excuse himself with "I am not well."

Ambika touched his forehead which was feverish. The two sisters decided to report it to Satyavati against his wish and despite his protests.

However, before she could be informed, Satyavati was there, fairly concerned about her son. She called for the state physician and ordered his wives to give him a massage. But he withdrew his feet in resistance. When asked why, he told his mother that it increased his temperature.

Satyavati was dumbfounded at the revelation. His wives' touch increased his temperature! Vichitravirya was so intensely passionate.

The Rajavaidya examined Vichitravirya and reported his condition to Satyavati.

"The king is overly passionate. He is physically very weak. And you have provided him not one but two beautiful wives," he explicitly remarked.

"I detect symptoms of tuberculosis in the king. I had requested you to keep him off sensual acts. I had made it quite clear to the senior prince that even one wife could be detrimental to his health. Still he was given two queens. A king having two queens is not wrong but our king is an exception. His proximity could infect the queens and deteriorate his condition too."

Satyavati cursed herself. What was her fault? What sin had she committed that she was being punished? First, she was separated from her beloved recluse, then she had to abandon her little Krishna Dvaipayana, then she had to marry an old man and was widowed, then she lost her elder son, Chitrangada, and now it was Vichitravirya. Was it because she and her foster father, her Baba, craved for kingdom or because she hijacked Bhishma's right to rule? Was it her own doing or someone else's? Was it divine or man-made?

Satyawati was baffled. Why should it all happen to her? The Rajavaidya told her that he had cautioned Bhishma that even one wife could spell disaster to Vichitravirya. Why was Bhishma then so persistent upon getting Vichitravirya married? Was there some design behind that? Did he want to exploit his weakness for the feminine flesh and thus accelerate his ruin?

Bhishma was out to finish her child, Satyavati concluded, and decided to visit Bhishma.

At Bhishma's palace, Satyavati was informed that he was in dialogue with Virsen, the charioteer, who was just back from Sobha.

In Bhishma's chamber, her eyes met Amba's who was visibly distraught after a long tedious journey.

How come she was there? Satyavati wondered as she was supposed to be at Sobha.

Amba, disregarding Satyavati, neither addressed nor saluted her. When Satyavati queried Bhishma, he whispered:

"Yes, mother! Shalva has refused to take her in. He says when he could not win her in combat, he would not accept her as a dole from Bhishma."

"Why don't you speak out the whole truth?" said Amba, at once angry and pathetic. "Listen to me, queen mother," she turned to Satyavati, "He says that the moment Bhishma caught me and seated me upon his chariot, I became Bhishma's wife," and Shalva would not accept me as his own wife. Shalva would not commit adultery.

"This can't be!" Satyavati rebuffed. "Bhishma is pledged to a life-long celibacy. He abducted you for his younger brother Vichitravirya. You yourself admitted to have secretly chosen King Shalva of Sobha. Otherwise, you would have been married to Vichitravirya and been the queen of the Kuru empire."

"Which I still am!" Amba insisted. "But I am the wife of Devavrata Bhishma, the son of Shantanu. The Hastinapur royalty must accept me as such."

Satyavati turned to Bhishma in dismay. "Patience, mother," Bhishma came forward to assuage Satyavati's frayed sentiments. He tried to convince her that Amba's outburst was but an outcome of her agitated mind, her affliction.

"Don't try to cajole me," Amba interrupted him. "If you are a kshatriya, I am also the daughter of a kshatriya. If you are firm in your pledge, I will also realise what I have resolved."

"I have not done you any wrong by abducting you. Your manifestation of love for Shalva was not wrong. And Shalva's denial of you was also not wrong," asserted Bhishma.

"When no wrong was committed by anyone and no one was wrong, why only I should be subjected to this?" Amba protested. "I was abducted from my home so I cannot return there. My abductor would not accept me for he is bound in his pledge of celibacy. And he who loved and wished to marry me could not take me because he could not abduct me. When everyone was just in his act, why should I endure all this tyranny alone? Why don't you wander about in woods and towns like me?"

Bhishma readily regretted her plight and offered to help her out. He said, "If you wish to return to your paternal home or if you wish to marry Vichitravirya…, whatever."

Even as Satyavati was alarmed by that proposition which she considered fatal for Vichitravirya, Amba protested, "I don't desire to return to my parental home. I don't desire to marry the impotent Vichitravirya and I don't desire to stay in Hastinapur as a Kuru woman nor do I desire to go to King Shalva of Sobha."

"What do you desire then?"

"I must be accepted by the one whose wife I am, otherwise..."

"Otherwise?"

"Otherwise, Bhishma, I will revenge my insult through some terrific act." And she threatened to annihilate the entire stock of "this one woman for whose pleasure you intend to ruin my life."

Satyavati was terrified. Amba appeared to be a cursed,

restive spirit who was out to marry Bhishma and install herself as the queen of Hastinapur and Bhishma as the king, and possibly assassinate Vichitravirya andmay be even Bhishma.

The answer came from Bhishma who declared: "I will not be able to do your wish in this birth at least."

When Bhishma refused to relent, Amba asked to be taken to Shaikhavatya muni's ashram, so that she could start preparing for the destruction of Hastinapur.

As for Ambika and Ambalika, they were fairly aware of their elder sister's presence in Hastinapur and were concerned why she had not cared to meet them. In their discourse, Ambika sounded the wiser one.

They talked about Bhishma, about Shalva, and about Vichitravirya. Their conversation ended with Ambika observing that often ignorance was more blissful than knowledge.

28

The first one to visit Bhishma that morning was Rajavaidya, the royal physician. He informed Bhishma of Vichitravirya's critical state and complained that, as a sick man, he was not under his control. The king's will was supreme, the physician regretted.

"Now is the time you understood the status of the king's physique and ailment," the royal physician implored. "He is not only ignoring his condition but also being atrocious to himself. A physician's duty is to diagnose and treat, not to reign in the kings. I am, thus, here to inform you that the king's condition is out of my hand. If you can handle him, I am still sure I will handle his disease."

"Did you tell the queen mother?" Bhishma enquired, though he knew it was easier said than done. He knew she would not be able to endure the shock of such a cruel news. Sometimes, Bhishma, like children, fantasised about a fairy-world where no one ever suffered where there was no hatred, greed, malice and fear, where everyone loved everyone else. Why couldn't God create such a world, Bhishma grieved? What would he lose?

But this was no time for solving any philosophical riddles. It was time to care for Vichitravirya's health and inform mother Satyavati.

Presently, Bhishma was informed of the arrival of two brahmacharis (celibates) from the ashram of Mahatharvana Jabali. They declared that they were there with a piece of good news for Bhishma.

"We have received this news at our ashram from the ashram of your mentor Mahabhargava Bhagvan Parashurama that he will come to our ashram beside the holy Sarasvati in Kurukshetra and he will like to see you. But, as he will not enter Hastinapur, he wants you to be at Kurukshetra."

This was a pleasant surprise for Bhishma as he never had an opportunity to revisit Parashurama's ashram since his departure from there.

"I will definitely see him," Bhishma said. "It is my luck that he remembered me, though it would please me if he could come to Hastinapur." And he ordered the attendant to take proper care of them who were there "with my mentor's message."

That served as an excuse for informing Queen Mother Satyavati of Vichitravirya's critical condition as well.

He apprised Satyavati of Parashurama's arrival and said, "I would like to start for Kurukshetra tomorrow. I may take two or three days. You may, please, look after Vichitravirya's health. The Rajavaidya says that the king is not in his control and therefore not in control of the medicine. If things don't improve, it will be an alarming situation for the king even Ashivini Kumara (the great legendary physician) would not be able to do anything for him."

As an afterthought, Satyavati spoke out to Bhishma, "I have heard both Parashurama and Mahatharvana are great physicians. I will go with you and beg them for Vichitravirya's life. Maybe the royal physician is lacking in something. Let us exploit their unforeseen presence."

Bhishma wanted to vehemently protest and say that neither was the royal physician a quack nor was there any dearth of medicines. But if a person in his sickness did not stick to a proper regimen, no physician could save him. But he said, "As you wish, mother."

29

It was not a pupil's journey to see his mentor. A large retinue accompanied Bhishma from Hastinapur. Satyavati was there to seek a cure for Vichitravirya who had to be left behind on the royal physician's advice. And thus Ambika and Ambalika were not taken along. Bhishma, Satyavati, the Prime Minister Vishnudutt and the royal priest Vasubhuti's chariots were followed by other carriages and wagons carrying attendants, soldiers and provisions. The whole get up, though, had been managed despite Bhishma who would rather meet his guru as a humble pupil.

Bhishma recalled that his mother Ganga had abandoned him in infancy and his father roamed hunting through forests, baffled and bewildered. Bhishma was reared and fostered at various ashrams. He was a case in himself, thus whiling away his time even as both his parents were well and alive.

Parashurama, as a mentor, was a strict disciplinarian. He would never tolerate a fault, however big or small. To him, every mistake deserved a punishment and not pardon. We must accept a penalty for our ill deeds as we expect a reward for our good deeds, was his motto. Though hard in his principles, Parashurama was soft and kind at heart.

Bhishma reminisced about his days spent under Parashurama's patronage. He remembered how the guru's benevolence was bestowed upon him, specially as he had to spend his vacations without a mate as all of his fellow-mates at the ashram would spend their vacations with their parents. He remembered how, at his departure, the venerable mentor's wife had insisted that "one home for you is the one where you were born and your second home is this ashram where you were trained. As you are drawn towards Hastinapur, so also remember this ashram." But, alas, Bhishma could not honour her words. Once in Hastinapur after years of roaming through various ashrams, he was stuck there for good.

On the way, near the ashram, the caravan was intercepted by four youths on horses, who turned out to be celibates sent to receive and inform them that the Bhagvan had already arrived and was waiting for them at the ashram.

Bhishma blushed at the thought that he was going to shoot arrows at them, who were actually there to escort them honourably and securely to his host's ashram. How could he forget that his mentor Mahabhargava was not an ordinary forest-dwelling recluse, but an expert in arms and master of warfare. He had the best and rarest breed of steed at his ashram. Even his ordinary pupils were ace equestrians.

They reached Parashurama's make-shift ashram beside the Sarasvati. It was more of a military cantonment guarded by armed celibates. Bhishma, Satyavati, Vishnudutt and Vasubhuti were escorted to where Parashurama waited for them.

Bhishma observed obvious changes in his guru. When Bhishma was an inmate of his ashram, Parashurama was young but now he was quite advanced in years. Bhishma bowed at Parashurama's feet in veneration.

After preliminary salutation, the guru exclaimed, "You quit the kingdom and you forsook the craving for a wife and children. Son, if salt and sweet are taken out of food, all other tastes are left out by themselves. Similarly if wealth and woman are disparaged, all other attachments in life lose their import. Don't you feel so?"

Bhishma said, "As for now, I feel I have consciously suppressed all the mean sentiments that raise their head at the slightest laxity. I am still not liberated from any of them."

"Never mind!" Parashurama remarked. "You still have a lot of time left with you. Be firm in your dharma for I have summoned you to test just that." His smile was enigmatic.

Satyavati, along with Vasubhuti and Vishnudutt, was introduced to Parashurama and was fairly impressed by his grandeur.

In the evening, at the assembly hall, Bhishma could discern much more than was apparent. Those gathered there included Shaikhavatya the sage and King Hotravahan, the maternal grandfather of Amba, the princess of Kashi.

Alarm bells rang in Bhishma's head, particularly at the mention of the latter. So it was all to do with her!

"Devavrata!" the guru said, "Your renown rests on your renunciation. Of course, there are others who live without a kingdom and woman, but the way you have renounced the readily available enjoyments is laudable. I am pleased by the fact that the royalty has not overwhelmed you. Incidentally, I hope your vow was taken so that the impediments in the way of the accomplishment of your father's aspiration could be dispelled!"

"Yes, gurudeva!"

"Which means you did it for others' sake; you had no stake in it; you recognised dharma in your affliction. It follows that you adopted this element of dharma that you will not seek your own interest while practising altruism..." At that juncture someone made a dramatic appearance. It was Amba!

'So she is also here,' said Bhishma to himself, trying to recover from that recent jolt.

All was clear to him now. So it was all planned for her! Apparently Amba went to her grandfather, King Hotravahana, who took her to Shaikhavatya the sage, and the sage saw her only possible salvation in the guru's command.

As Amba sat down, Parashurama returned to Bhishma. "When you had abducted her from the swayamvara, why didn't you marry her?" he quizzed Bhishma.

"Due to my vow of celibacy."

"But you didn't make that announcement at the swayamvara."

"Kashiraja's bard did it."

"You did not endorse that but you declared you were abducting the princesses, which could well imply that the abduction was your way of protest. If Amba concluded you were abducting her to wed her, what would you say to that?"

"Her illusion."

"Shouldn't you have rectified that?"

"Will you not concede the benefit of doubt in my case, great master?"

"But your insignificant error is going to ruin this girl's life. Shalva didn't accept her for he considers her your wife because you abducted her. She is being made the victim of the tussle between you and Shalva. I cannot allow this excess against her. You must accept her."

"The present dilemma is the consequence of a lack of fidelity in the princess. Otherwise, Shalva or Vichitravirya..."

"She desires you as her husband,not Vichitravirya."

"Which is not possible in this life, great master."

"Now if you marry Amba to save her from ruin, it would be an act of gratefulness," said Parashurama.

Satyavati was virtually on the verge of an outburst. She was inclined to say, "No, great sage! Don't be so reckless. This Amba is not a princess but a nagin (female cobra), who is born to finish Satyavati. If she married Bhishma … The rival parties would not be Bhishma and Amba, but Satyavati and Amba, and the kingdom would be Bhishma! The woman who will have Bhishma will also acquire the absolute kingdom of Hastinapur. Satyavati has Bhishma as her son and Amba craves to have him as her spouse. I know by instinct that a man is more under the sway of his wife than his mother. As a mother, a woman has always lost the contest. Protect Amba's rights, O great sage, but also do not deprive me of mine…"

But Satyavati realized that it was still not an opportune moment to say that when Bhishma himself was defying his guru, who presently exhorted,"Your father didn't even order you to, but it was of your own will that you forsook all material pleasure once you knew his desire. The guru wields more authority than the father. This is my order: Accept Amba. Enjoy the pleasures of the household and make her happy."

"If I don't find myself competent enough to obey your order?"

"It is not expected of the pupils of the gurukula to disobey their guru. If you violate, I will have to compel you to obey me. I may even have to resort to arms. Will you fight with your guru?"

Fight with the guru! That was frankly a dangerous proposition. If Bhishma lost the fight with his guru, an old brahmin, he would be too humiliated to show his face to his community. Andif he defeated his guru and was forced to kill him, he would be condemned for a brahmin's murder!

"Why did dharma prescribe arms for a kshatriya?" Bhishma begged Parashurama's verdict.

"To deliver justice. It is banditry to wear arms to fulfill one's own selfish ends."

"Not to thrust one's will upon others?"

"No. It behoves an oppressor. Dharma does not permit that."

"Why should you then resort to arms to thrust your and the princess' will upon me? What dharma do you uphold by lifting your bow to get the princess marry me?"

"To protect a women's honour is every man's dharma, Devavrata Bhishma. Either you accept Amba as your wife or you pay for the non-compliance with your life. Pick up your bow."

"Wait, gurudeva! Let me first be convinced of the inevitability of the combat. Besides if I do your bidding, how do I honour my vow?"

"You should have contemplated that when you abducted Amba. Just as you took a vow I took another vow-to help the helpless. You are my pupil and, thus, you have to be all the more conscious. I will never let it come to pass that you don't defend a woman's dignity. I am the defender of the one who is defenceless."

As a last desperate effort to salvage the crisis, Bhishma offered a safe and reputable refuge to Amba in Hastinapur but she declined it outright.

"No! I don't need one," she cried out.

At that point Hotrivahana intervened, saying, "Let it not be perceived that Amba is without any custodian and she needs any refuge. She can go back to her father. She can reside with me. She can dwell at the sage Shaikhavatya's ashram. It is in fact a matter of her life's import and dignity. A young woman's life is not passed meaningfully at her father's or maternal grandfather's. It is essential that she get a loving husband so that her life attains significance and continuance in her children." Here he turned to Bhishma before resuming, "The question is, is the Kuru prince willing to accept her as his wife? If yes, I have nothing more to say. If no, Amba's life will be ruined. In that case, the Kuru prince will be guilty of snuffing a promising life, for which he must be punished."

Parashurama asked Bhishma if he would accept Amba as his wife.

"I am bound by my pledge not to," said Bhishma and was challenged by the guru to pick up his bow. Bhishma did that reluctantly and insisted, "I am not guilty, gurudeva. Moreover, I will not kill my preceptor." But Parashurama ignored his plea and trained his bow at Bhishma who was not the least hesitant to reciprocate.

It was Jabali's turn to intervene. "Is combat inevitable?" Jabali wanted to know from the guru.

"Yes!"

"Is Bhishma the culprit?"

"Yes!"

"Will killing Bhishma avenge the injustice?"

"There is no option."

"Will it fulfill the princess' wish?"

Parashurama realised he was still in two minds. Was he killing Bhishma for justice's sake or was he bound by his tenets, offering to act as a means of wish-fulfilment for Amba?

Instinctively, Satyavati came upto Parashurama and stood before him in supplication. "O great sage," she said. "What is dharma, you know well. I am an ignorant worldly woman. Still I may assure you that Amba's life will not be wasted. I offer to be both her mother-in-law by her marriage to Vichitravirya and her mother. If she declines both the options, she is not helpless or without a guardian. She is a witch out to devastate Hastinapur and you are playing in her hands with your blind faith in justice. Don't you perceive she is after Bhishma in her lust? She will not settle for anything less. She is not insisting on justice but on lust. I had come here to beg you for Vichitravirya's life, whereas you seem keen to take away even Bhishma from me."

Parashurama watched her stupefied. He became pensive and slackened his grip on the bow.

Bhishma would not lose chance to strike when the iron was hot. "O great preceptor," he said, "I am not responsible for Amba's present predicament. I am not guilty in her case. She confessed her love and attachment for Shalva and abandoned her gain of her own will."

Parashurama turned to Amba, "Anything from your side?"

"I will also beg amnesty for a moment's frailty, O great sage! In that moment of frailty, I perceived Bhishma's vow as an impregnable iron wall and, to escape Vichitravirya, went to Shalva. But Shalva's disapproval exposed both my vulnerable position and my desire to me."

The aged prime minister of Hastinapur, Vishnudutt, stepped in with Parashurama's proper permission. "The Hastinapur empire and the royal Kuru dynasty rests on Bhishma's muscle power, and Bhishma is the plank of the people's faith across this region. No doubt, I will be the most pleased by Bhishma's marriage, but tell me if Bhishma broke his pledge, who will the common Aryavata man trust?"

Parashurama was perceptibly perturbed. He turned to Amba to ask whether she would like a dignified settlement of her life or Bhishma?

"Bhishma," came the apt response from her. "Bhishma is mine. The kingdom of Hastinapur is mine. I will not take anything less."

"It's not possible at least in this life," Bhishma said.

Amba conceded to wait for a next life. "In this life you will either be mine or you will lose your life," she asserted.

Parashurama took strong exception to Amba's last statement and declared decisively, "I will not be able to help you in any manner. Now you may carry on your efforts through another medium. Hotiavahana!" he turned to Amba's grandfather, "take along Amba with you. Parashurama is saved from a great sin this day."

"Bhishma!" Amba spoke in a trembling voice, "I will burn myself in penance so that your life, that was not to be mine, could be consumed."

"I will be sorry, O princess!"

"I will die with a wish to finish this physical frame of yours, which impedes our union. Justice is not begged; It has to be taken," said Amba and went out.

Bhishma observedAmba for some time. She was, of course, sad but he did not hold himself responsible for her condition. But he was indebted to her. He must allow her a chance to calm down. Could he say that he and Amba would not be bound to each other in their future births?

Bhishma could not rule out that possibility.

30

On her way back to Hastinapur, Satyavati was lost in a confused welter of emotions. She did not know if she was glad or not. When she had journeyed to Kurukshetra, her sole intent was to seek some potion, learn some magic formula (mantra) from Bhagvan Parashurama and Mahatharvana Jaboli for her son Vichitravirya. But that was not to be. Instead she had ended up pleading with Parashurama to spare Bhishma's life.

Actually Bhishma's defeat and death by Parashurama would have cost her nothing. In fact Bhishma's existence made her guilty in others' eyes. More so, it would not have settled the riddle of Amba, who was not out for Bhishma's demise anyway. And if Amba could win over Bhishma, she would certainly claim Hastinapur. If a humble Nishada girl, which Satyavati basically was, could not help herself succumb to the lure of kingdom, would Amba, a princess, let any such opportunity go by? Never.

But what about Bhishma's pledge? Satyavati laughed at the thought. A man's pledge, what did it mean? It is the woman who makes him take a pledge or even break it. If Satyavati, a mother, could prompt Bhishma into such a vow, could not Amba as a wife have him revoke it? If not Bhishma, Satyavati was definitely aware of the woman's power. A woman could prevail over a man's life just as the intoxicating season of spring and consume his conscience and resolve. A woman could gnaw into his roots like a termite and the man became aware only after his roots were completely destroyed and he fell down. Satyavati herself had overpowered and captivated Shantanu, who was by no standard a weak-willed man. If she had conceded to his way, Chitrangada and Vichitravirya would not have been brought up the way they were. He would have dispatched them to some gurukula, and by the time they would come back, Bhishma would have established himself as the popular king of Hastinapur, and the two younger brothers would have surrendered absolutely to his will. They would have grown up to be sons of a sage and not princes.

However, Satyavati did not let Shantanu have his way. A man was what he was only till the woman would not march out to vanquish him. By saving Bhishma from Amba's attraction, Satyavati had protected herself and Vichitravirya. What if she could not procure a potion or incantation for Vichitravirya, she had brought back the shield of defence, that Bhishma was, for her son.

The moment Satyavati arrived in Hastinapur, she was apprised of Vichitravirya's deteriorating condition and the treatment he was receiving. The king was not well, she was told.

She rushed into his chamber and found him on his bed surrounded by the royal physician and his assistants and pupils. In a corner sat Ambika and Ambalika, unconcerned as usual and apparently compelled by decorum. She had never appreciated their resigned altitude. Amba was far better than them in that she never concealed her love or hatred for anyone.

Satyavati approached Vichitravirya who looked morbid and pale. She looked askance at the royal physician, who said, "We are doing our best, Queen Mother, but we are not much hopeful." She had to struggle hard to hold back her anger. She could have hit her head against a wall or anyone confronting her at the moment.

During such an episode she was always reminded of Bhishma, who she perceived behind all that was happening to her and hers. She thought he always knew her children would never occupy the throne and had, therefore, so readily adopted the vows.

And then the blow! The royal physician gestured to his pupil who covered the king's face with a cloth. The physician sat down on the floor before the Queen Mother and declared, "The King is no more." The royal physician was joined by his assistants and pupils who all sat down upon the ground in front of Satyavati, who was spun around by a whirlwind of assumptions.

Bhishma must have known the future events, she thought. He must have known that both Chitrangada and Vichitravirya would soon pass away. Bhishma's retiring to a cottage for penance after Shantanu's demise, wasn't it one of his humbugs? Was he not then evoking magic to kill Chitrangada? He was familiar with that tradition of hocus-pocus. No wonder, it was all a consequence of his experiments with that craft. All those who could obstruct his path had died one by one, be it Shantanu, Chitrangada, or Vichitravirya! Was his visit to Kurukshetra in the presence of his preceptor Parashurama and Jabali also not designed? Hadn't he organised some ritual beside the Sarasvati that incapacitated the royal physician and his assistants and they could do nothing to cure Vichitravirya, whose condition worsened with every dose they administered to him? Otherwise why did the best of medication fail? Wasn't it why Bhishma had slipped away to Kurukshetra exactly when Vichitravirya would be embraced by death? So that his absence from Hastinapur would stand testimony to Bhishma's innocence. How well planned and executed!

Fear shook her to the bones. She was surrounded by her enemies and trapped in the fishing net. A boatman's daughter, Satyavati best understood the plight of a fish caught in the net. The fishermen whom she was looking up for aid were actually her killers.

Satyavati never knew that she, a fisherwoman from the Yamuna riverside, would herself be made a fish in Hastinapur. These people had killed Vichitravirya; they could kill Satyavati as well.

Even otherwise, there was nothing in Hastinapur now that she could call her own. The king whose consort she was and the two kings whose mother she was were all dead. She was no more a queen or a mother queen. She had no emblem of authority in Hastinapur now. Why should anyone obey her now? Would Bhishma force her into exile from Hastinapur? Where would she go? To her Baba, who must be older and weaker now, unable to support her? Would she be able to resume her vocation of charitable ferrying, to cast and draw the net?

Where would she tarry? Krishna Draipayana! Could Krishna Dvaipayana's ashram be home to her? But he

was a hermit, dwelt in cottages, roamed through forests and mountains, and spends his time in meditation. Howsoever uncomfortable his abode, his mere thought was a harbinger of security. But would he be any match to Bhishma? That was a vital question. What if Bhishma decided to kill him too?

That was not so very likely, Satyavati convinced herself. Her Krishna was quite so different. He was a brahmin and Bhishma would never kill a brahmin. More so, Krishna did not reside in the palaces of Hastinapur. He did not depend on the royal physician's medicine. And, as for the magical tricks and rituals, Krishna himself was well-trained. Why, she should have remembered him earlier!

Satyavati surveyed the scene. Several prominent people were already there. Quite a presence. Among them, of course, was Bhishma whose supremacy was self-evident, and recognised by all and sundry. How imposing! Fighting bereavement. Must be secretly pleased that the kingdom was now his. The kingdom smeared in his brothers' blood.

What joy would he derive from this kingdom?

Satyavati detected Ambika and Ambalika who were still sitting dumbly in a corner. What would be their lot, she wondered, for they were in the same boat now as she was. Their consort, the king was also no more. They had no son either. Would Bhishma expel them too? Kill them or marry them? Yes, the last was also likely. As Bhishma had abducted them, no one from the kshatriya community would censure him. He would be the prime choice for kingship. Then, the kingdom and the queens both would be Bhishma's. And in that scenario he could not resist his marriage with Amba who also he had abducted and who was, anyway, performing penance in some nearby forest.

Her pent-up grief exploded as they carried Vichitravirya's body out of the premises.

At Bhishma's behest, they stopped so that Satyavati could have a last glimpse of the deceased. Bhishma consoled her.

"Mother! Patience! We can't do anything against His
will."

"Patience! Whose presence will now appeal patience from me?"

"Why, I am there, mother! Your bereaved son! You are there, I am there and so are these consorts of Vichitravirya! We are each other's support in these moments of grief!"

Satyavati watched him in awe. Was his grief genuine? Why should he be in grief?

Satyavati had always been apprehensive of Bhishma's intent. Now too. At most times, however, she had been proved wrong.

At Shantanu's demise, for instance, she had feared her expulsion from Hastinapur. But, she was saved, so she thought, by her own son. From a queen, she was upgraded to the status of a queen mother. Couldn't it be repeated with Ambika and Ambalika?

Why not! She saw her solution in Krishna Dvaipayana. He was, like Chitrangada and Vichitravirya, the queen mother's son. He had all the right to be a king. She would coronate him herself.

As usual, though, Bhishma stood in her imagination, all attired as a warrior. He looked at her with contempt and hit Krishna Dvaipayna with his sword. Krishna Dvaipayana's head rolled down on the ground; his severed torso stayed on the throne for a brief while and came down.

Wide-eyed Satyavati looked on and then exclaimed, "Why, Bhishma, you murdered a Brahmin!"

"He was not a Brahmin but a bandit who was unlawfully occupying the throne of the Kurus. It is the moral duty of a Kshatriya to kill a bandit."

"But he was the king of Hastinapur."

"No way. He was not a Kuru."

"So what. He was my son-the erstwhile king's brother."

"But not Shantanu's son, a pre-requisite for occupying this throne, which only I am now."

"And what about your vow?"

"Which vow?"

"That you were abdicating"

"A king can abandon the throne but the throne will not abandon the king. The throne of Hastinapur must be occupied by a son of Shantanu."

"But you promised me that Hastinapur would be ruled by Vichitravirya and his sons' generations."

"I stick to that."

"Then the Kuru land will be ruled by Vichitravirya's son?"

"Yes! But where is he?"

The imagined conversation snapped with Bhishma's deafening guffaw.

In fact, a messenger from Bhishma was there to request her presence to pay her last tribute to the deceased king. She was stirred out of her reverie and prepared to go.

Ambika was at once conscious of the pink fading from Ambalika's cheeks. She was evidently scared.

"Why Ambalika?"

"I am awfully frightened, Didi."

"Why?"

"Because the king has left us."

"Why should you lament? Did he give you any pleasure that will be denied to you now?"

"No Didi. It's not about pleasure. I fear something untoward is going to happen," Ambalika's lips trembled as she spoke.

"What untoward you fear Ambalika! We were abducted against our will from our father's palace. Against our will were we handed over to an ailing lecher who was physically incapable of giving or getting any pleasure. You may call his death untoward or emancipating."

"So his death matters nothing to you!" Ambalika was astonished at what her elder sister said.

"It may matter to one who was alive. I feel I am a lifeless one without any will that could matter. I have learnt it by experience that the princesses are lifeless objects won in a war and can be bartered at comfort."

"It was all Bhishma's doing. It seems he was out to get a wife for everyone in the world. Had he got married in time, he would have been a father now and would have no headache to find anyone a wife," Ambalika blurted out.

"And I feel it was the queen mother Satyavati's greed for kingdom that brought us to our present plight. It was she who snared Bhishma and bound him up in those suffocating vows. All the time is he conscious of a breach."

"What will they do to us, Didi? Will they demand us to be a sati (who is burnt at her husband's pyre)?" Ambalika was scrupulous.

"Do you fear death?"

"Why, don't you?"

"No," Ambika asserted. "I wish to be left alone like a lifeless object or to be granted a right to die."

"You wish to die!"

"Yes! And you wish to live?"

"Can't say! But I am afraid of dying."

"I know not what I will be losing when I die."

"You desire nothing?"

"No, what do we gain from a desire? It is due to the desires that our queen mother has brought on herself such a calamity. And on us as well."

"What would she do then?"

"Hand over the kingdom to Bhishma and retire to a forest."

"Don't tell!"

"I'm right, Ambalika! Life is vain. And we have no authority over anything. I have closed my eyes from every likelihood. If the queen mother still considers us of any worth, she may cherish us. Otherwise we may get orders to immolate ourselves as sati."

Ambalika was horrified to paleness.

31

After much deliberation, Satyavati decided to have a word with Bhishma. She would not let life slip away from her grip so abruptly.

She called for Bhishma.

"The Kuru's throne stands vacant now," she indicated, "is it the end of the Bharata dynasty?"

"The assembly is convened. I will place the matter for deliberation. There is no heir in King Shantanu's line now. Let the Kuru chiefs and the kings of the Bharata take a stand."

"And you? Aren't you a descendant of King Shantanu?" The fearful proposition was finally out.

"I am, of course. But my vow binds me. And why should we take up an issue that defies solution?"

"Despite all consequences, even at the cost of my heart-break!"

"For me, truth is supreme, mother. I will not forsake truth, whose observance is dharma, the ethos. Self-interest has to be put behind if we would uphold dharma which is essential," Bhishma asserted.

"If your father's kingdom was being ruined in front of you, what would be the worth of your life, Bhishma?"

"Still truth is supreme to me."

"Truth does not depend on one vow," Satyavati contended. "You remember just one vow and ignore the other one."

"Which one?"

"You promised that Hastinapur will be ruled by the descendants of Vichitravirya?"

"But Vichitravirya has left none," Bhishma was puzzled.

"Why he has left two queens-young, beautiful, and fecund! If you will, they can still produce the heir to the throne of Hastinapur." Bhishma stood speechless beholding Satyavati, who appeared to him shorn of all regal dignity or grace, a mere woman of earthly considerations and cunning.

A base man is just like that, Bhishma thought, he creates and breaks rules for his convenience to realise his desires. For him external laws of nature don't exist and no adversity arises when they are violated.

Presently he said, "Mother! Ethics prescribes niyoga (the system of begetting children from a childless widow) under such circumstances. You may appoint some virtuous, learned and righteous brahmin for the purpose. He may produce Vichitravirya's heir from his field."

"And if I appoint you?"

"In that case, not Vichitravirya's but Bhishma's offspring will occupy the throne," Bhishma was blunt. "We have to work out a settlement where Vichitravirya's offspring hold the regal authority and Bhishma is not forced to deviate from truth. The appointee for niyoga must be an unknown man, who is possibly not allowed a second contact with her. Otherwise, the dharma would be violated and defiled. Let us not do that, mother!"

Satyavati's self was split in two. One said, "Enough is enough, Satyavati. You have struggled hard against his will. The enjoyment of regal amenities was not provided for your offspring. Let his will prevail. Hand over this kingdom to Bhishma, and Vichitravirya's wives too. Let go of all this. Leave the path of contention. Have peace."

But the other self condemned the counterpart,

"'Satyavati's striving and sacrificing was no less. Why should she surrender all the pleasures of life, even the two youthful and beautiful wives of Vichitravirya to Bhishma? No, she will never allow that. Not in any case. If she must appoint an unknown brahmin, why not her own Dvaipayana! What if she could not provide him the mundane pleasures of life, she will compensate it this way, now!"

But there was another hurdle! "Ambika and Ambalika's wish" as Bhishma proposed. "How does their will matter here?" Satyavati questioned. "Should the Kuru's heir wait for their will? Now you will suggest their consent be sought in the matter of appointing that man too, so that they may invite their erstwhile paramours and defile the throne of Hastinapur by installing their illicit offspring thus produced there!"

"That's definitely not what I mean. But, at least, they should be willing to procreate. They should be prepared to accept the appointed man as the will of the dharma."

"Did you consider their will when you decided to abduct them?" This one was rather hard to swallow for Bhishma.

"That was emergent, mother!"

"So is this, son. I must have a grandson and only Vichitravirya's consorts can produce him. And produce they must."

Bhishma could discern some reason in her plea! "That's fine, mother," he mildly submitted. "Don't ask for their will. Appoint some righteous, high-bred brahmin."

"No, not a Brahmin," protested Satyavati.

"Then?"

"You shall impregnate them."

It was a stinger this time.

"I don't have the power to realise the impossible, mother, nor have you."

The ensuring discourse tested the resolve of both Satyavati and Bhishma.

"Bhishma," Satyavati eventually proposed, "if you don't do my bidding to perform the act, you will have to endorse the man I will appoint. Will you?"

"I will, mother!"

"Even in the face of all objections?"

"Yes, mother!"

"Then I appoint the Mahamuni Krishna Dvaipayana Vedvyasa."

"Vedvyasa! Parashara's son!" Bhishma looked awkwardly at Satyavati. "Will he accept the invite?"

"Yes."

"How can you be so sure, mother?"

"Any objections?"

"No! If he accepts, I will have no objection."

"He will accept."

"You look so certain. How?"

"If I tell you the truth, will you respect me the less?"

"Nothing will ever diminish a son's regard for his mother."

"Bhishma! I am the mother of that son of Parashara's. He is my illicit son."

The revelation came as a pleasant surprise to Bhishma, who at once exclaimed, "Vedvyasa is a brother to me!"

"Yes, my son, from my side he is your brother."

"Let him accomplish the act (of niyoga) then," Bhishma said.

"Invite him, he will come."

32

Satyavati greeted the entry of Mahamuni (the great sage) Krishna Dvaipayana Vyasa with great alacrity. She looked up most affectionately and, at once, lowered her eyes perhaps in guilt. He was Satyavati's son who she had abandoned with his father at the time of birth.

As he sprinkled some water on her from his kamandala (a mendicant's wooden pot) and blessed her, Satyavati was taken aback. Should she hug him as his son or bow to him in veneration as a great sage?

Here he was: weather-beaten, tanned, tall and elderly, with graying hair and clad in valkala (tree-bark). His large sleepy eyes and the pout confirmed his identity.

The solitude commanded and the guest honourably seated, Satyavati proceeded, "Mahamuni, did the great sage Parashara ever tell you about your mother?"

"Yes, mother! The world may not, but I do know you are my mother. That's why I honoured your command at once. The fact was closely guarded as my father believed its disclosure might harm you."

Satyavati was overwhelmingly moved and embraced him. She was not pleased by the way Parashara had reared him. He looked rough and tough, so unlike his two princely brothers.

"Son! Your father reared you so roughly!" She could not hold herself back.

Vyasa smiled, "Yes, mother! You can't practise penance in delicacy."

"Did you ever think of me?"

"A great lot in childhood, mother, when I saw other

children in the company of their mothers."

"Then?"

"Then I befriended Mother Nature."

'So very like Parashara!' thought Satyavati.

"And then, I got to know mother Sarasvati."

"You must have cursed me for my cruelty that made me abandon you."

Vyasa smiled, "No, mother! Never."

"You love me?"

"Why shouldn't a son love his mother?"

"Why did you not reproach me then for my having deprived you?"

"What deprivation? You have fulfilled all my needs, mother!"

"Me?"

"Yes! You kept me in your womb. You brought me into this world. And then you handed me over to my father for rearing and learning. A greater love than this is only delusion. Where is the deprivation in this?"

"You borrowed these ideas from your father?" Tears appeared in Satyavati's eyes.

"These were taught to me by him and my experience has confirmed them."

Satyavati saluted Parashara for his sublime teachings to their son.

"How long will be your stay at Hastinapur?" she asked.

"Not so long as this is an unplanned visit. Please tell me why you have called me, mother! A mendicant must anyway stay away from places of indulgence, and royal palaces are the very hub of revelries! This place is not for me and I am not for this place."

"What fault do you find in a royal palace, son?"

"There is no fault in any object or place, mother! Only that every object and place has an essential attribute. The royalty represents passion, which would obstruct my path to seeking truth. A man has to recognise his nature, fix his goal. Accordingly does he tread the path to a courtesan's residence or a god's temple. Now, what prompted you to call me, pray?"

"My son! Chitrangada was the first to go, now Vichitravirya has also left us. Bhishma will not rule or marry for he is bound by his vow. There is no heir to Shantanu's dynasty nor a king for Hastinapur. I wish to appoint you to produce children from Vichitravirya's queens. Both my daughters-in-law are beautiful and youthful."

"These attributes are insignificant to me, mother! Now I am not governed by passion but dharma, which is not impressed by a woman's charm or tender age."

Upon insistence, though, he submitted, "Let the elder queen refrain from all indulgence for a year and dedicate herself to meditation and virtuousness."

"Krishna!" Satyavati implored, "we just can't afford to wait that long! The throne cannot be left vacant for any longer."

"In that case, you may inform me after she has bathed post her menstruation period. She should wait for me in her bed chamber not persuaded by a carnal desire but by a pious will to procreate. I will present myself in an unhandsome appearance, which should not repulse her. I will be motivated by dharma (sacred thoughts) and not sensual desire. Let her pray to God for a child through me. I believe, the Bharata lineage will not go barren, mother."

And Vyasa prepared to leave.

"Have you got married, son?" Satyavati could not help asking him.

"Yes, mother! Maha-atharvana Jabali's daughter Vatika is my wife and I have a small son named Shukra."

Vyasa departed, leaving a doleful Satyavati behind.

33

Ambika sat admiring her own reflection in the mirror and was thrilled. Why, she was young, and beautiful too! She could still charm and captivate a man! Her beauty was her priceless asset which must be carefully cherished. Wasn't it by her charm that mother Satyavati had first disarmed King Shantanu and then unnerved him. Only Satyavati's beauty had prevailed. A woman's beauty was an invaluable asset-the ultimate victor.

Ambika's desire to live was revived. There was so much to be enjoyed. Nature had created those pleasures so that no man could turn his back to them. Dejection was but inevitable and spared no one. But one should not retain it for long and try to drive it out of life. The vacuum created thus would soon be filled up by hope.

Until now, Ambika's experience had been otherwise. When the elder prince Bhishma had abducted her and the two sisters, she had trembled like Ambalika, and had closed her eyes at the blood-shed. Bhishma had, however, refrained from killing anyone, including Shalva, which convinced her Bhishma was not so cruel.

But wasn't it Bhishma's cruelty when he brought the three sisters to Hastinapur and dumped them at the feet of Vichitravirya? True to her nature, Amba had cleared herself of the mess and Ambika was left with the chicken-hearted Ambalika. Ambika would possibly have loved Vichitravirya who was good-looking, young, and her husband by social sanction. But he was so short-lived. Sensually aroused, he looked pitiable. Gradually she came to know that the man she and Ambalika had got as a husband was incapable of physical relations. Then Ambika realised that the royal palace at Hastinapur was vacant but for the queen mother Satyavati's aspirations. All were mere puppets of her will-even the elder prince, Bhishma.

When Vichitravirya died, Ambika thanked her stars that she had not been commanded to burn herself on her husband's pyre, which was otherwise a common practice. For Ambika, life had come to a halt at the end of a blind tunnel.

To her pleasant surprise the queen mother had started cajoling her into embracing a meaningful life. She persuaded Ambika to accept life as a challenge, to drag herself from the gloom which she had come to embrace as her fate. She had become oblivious of her beauty, her youth.

Ambika felt that within her was a vast cave, pitch dark and black, in which scenes of her past life were re-enacted as wounds and her mind flew as a crow from one wound to another. She never realised that a whole world existed outside the cave where sunset was followed by sunrise, darkness was followed by light, autumn was followed by spring; this world was laden with countless blossoms of myriad hues and luscious fruits appeared on trees. She never realised that outside the dark cave there existed open hills with springs of sweet water. That rivers flowed from those mountains and covered large expanse of land, quenching the thirst of the earth and blessing it with life. Yes, life! Why, she never thought about life; she was conscious of that dark cave only!

And one day the queen mother announced her wish for a grandson, which Ambika easily ignored as not concerning her. Why should she bother about Satyavati's grandson? Satyavati required several sons, she required a kingdom for her sons, the kingdom required an heir; to produce the heir, she required princesses; to abduct the princesses, she required Bhishma; to keep Bhishma bound, she required a vow; and consequent upon the vow, she required servants... Servants and even more servants, who would be her obedient puppets. The queen mother did not think that there were people in the world who were least interested in all these relations and objects, such pleasures never fascinated them. Vichitravirya had enjoyed those pleasures. What was his gain? Tuberculosis! People must live out the life destined for them. Why should they need sons and grandsons?

However, the next time the queen mother approached her, she talked not of her grandson but of Ambika's son, which her mind did not register! Ambika did not want a child nor was there any such likelihood.

"Don't you want a son? Aren't you a woman? Haven't you the slightest will to procreate?" the queen mother admonished her.

"Why should any woman desire a child, I just fail to understand," Ambika spoke slowly. "Retaining it in womb, delivering, then rearing, educating and fearing every moment for it... Why should people want a child? What do they get... what joy?"

This was a bolt from the blue for Satyavati, who retorted: "Why does one sow seeds? Why does a plant grow? Why is it shielded from extreme cold and sun? What joy does it provide? What comfort? One has to invest not only time and labour on it, but also money."

"That's what I think," Ambika said. "Why should one sow seeds? Maybe they have no other means to pass the time."

"Well, you may believe that," Satyavati asserted. "Why, you should also produce a son to pass the time."

A real shock and so exasperating. Did she really say that?

"I have no problem passing my time, queen mother!" Ambika confronted Satyavati. "Besides, is it any possible to produce a son when the king is no more?"

"Yes."

"How?"

"Through niyoga. Through another man appointed for that exclusive purpose."

Ambika was outraged: "I am neither a cow from your pen nor a machine to produce a grandson for you."

"My daughter!" Satyavati was mellowed this time. "Producing a child would not make a woman a cow or a machine! Procreation is a woman's cherished dharma. Which woman would deny procreation when feasible?"

That was not enough to convince Ambika though. "To love and marry a man and to produce children from him could be a matter of pride for a woman," she submitted. "But to bed a stranger for the sheer purpose of procreation is absurd!"

"No stranger is going to approach you. It is your own jyestha, your husband's elder brother," said Satyavati and promptly left.

When left to herself, Ambika came to terms with what was happening, what was going to happen. Satyavati's words haunted her: 'It is your jyestha.' The queen mother had already decided and there was no chance to dispute. The man had been appointed! She was bound to produce a grandson for the queen mother whose command was supreme in that family. The throne of Hastinapur could not remain vacant. Her own will did not matter at all. The birth of an heir was inevitable.

A sleepless night awaited Ambika. She thought about Vichitravirya, about Bhishma, about Bhishma's age, his celibacy, his appearance. Her sister Amba's choice was commendable. Shalva compared to Bhishma was like a mouse before a roaring lion. 'I would not kill the helpless,' he had said. How kind and brave at once!

The furrows on Bhishma's face were not because of years but circumstances. Despite his age, he still looked attractive. A woman would perhaps not greet a wrinkle on her own face, but would like a sign of maturity on a man's face.

Her nocturnal musings continued till dawn when she realised she must take care of her appearance. "I cannot be as unmindful as Bhishma is. It is creditable unto a woman to be able to attract a dispassionate man, whereas a dispassionate woman is likely to be forsaken by a man.'

Conscious of her appearance, Ambika started taking interest in her toiletries and dresses. Often she would walk out into the garden where she looked intently at pretty blossoms and, thrilled by their fragrance, she broke into a melody. Interestingly, Satyavati was aware of all that through scores of maids who spied for her. Satyavati had stocked heaps of cosmetics for Ambika's use and all efforts were on to increase her desire.

Suddenly, there was a great commotion. The maids and attendants scurried out of Ambika's chamber. Only Ambika's personal attendant was there to whisper to her, "Mistress! He is coming-the appointed one!"

And she hurried off too.

Amidst a frightening silence, Ambika heard steady footfall approaching her with a regular rhythm.

She did not dare to look up.

The sound was very close to her bed now. She was dying to hear a word, some word.

'Devi (dear lady)!" someone said at last.

Ambika looked up and her eyes saw a tall man, unlikeable and unhandsome at once.

"Who are you?" she managed to ask.

"Your husband's elder brother! The queen mother's illicit son, Vedvyasa. Ready for the niyoga, dear lady?"

Ambika wished to shout out her refusal, stand up, give a powerful push to the weird one, and rush out of her chamber.

But she could do nothing. She went numb and fell spiritless upon her bed.

She lay in an unprecedented state of despondence. She recalled her previous practice and closed her eyes. She would have been wise to remember that Bhishma had pledged celibacy and he would never break a vow.

34

When Vyasa approached Satyavati to seek her leave, tears welled up in her eyes.

"I wait for the moment you will come to stay with me," she said.

"That moment will never come, mother!"

"Which means we are destined to stay separately for good?"

"No way! We will stay together in all probability, but not here in this royal palace of Hastinapur. It will be at the sage Krishna Dvaipayana's ashram."

Satyavati changed the topic and asked, "was Ambika hospitable?"

"No, she was expecting someone else. She was disgusted to see me. She shut her eyes."

"Then?"

"She did not frustrate your plan, mother! You will be blessed with a grandson." Vyasa said, "but, she was not righteously inclined; sensual pleasure dominated her mind and, therefore, I fear your grandson may be a lecher."

Next Satyavati wanted to know if Vyasa had met Bhishma and how had he treated him.

"Most amicably! Most cordially!" Vyasa said.

Even constant prodding from Satyavati could not coerce Vyasa into censuring Bhishma on any account.

"My son, has Bhishma shed his animosity for me? Or will he ever be able to?"

"Mother! Bhishma has never been your enemy."

"Why did he decline the niyoga? Don't you think he is averse to Vichitravirya's heir taking birth?"

Vyasa laughed it off. He said, "you are so very innocent, mother. If Bhishma was averse, why should he greet me here?"

"Why did he decline the niyoga then?"

"To defend his pledge."

"Even at the cost of one's feelings? Even if it caused harm to one? The one who is harmed will surely consider him his enemy?"

"It is egoistic to judge the enmity and friendship against one's loss and gain, mother!" Vyasa said. "Friendship goes by spirit and not by deed."

"Bhishma is not my enemy, you say?"

"No."

"Since when?"

"He has never been your enemy."

"Why should I always feel so?"

"For you are Bhishma's enemy."

"But why should I be when he deprived me of nothing? On the other hand, I seized his kingdom; he should have been my enemy."

"Bhishma does not think his kingdom was seized; he believes he has abdicated."

"But who forced him to do that?"

"Bhishma does not recognise any force. He believes abdication is done by will."

"Why should one abdicate by will?"

"For the kingdom was superfluous to him. Renunciation of the superfluous unburdens a man."

"If that is his claim, he is lying because there cannot be a man who would not need a kingdom."

"I don't. Don't you believe me, mother?"

"But you are Parashara's son; Bhishma is King Shantanu's."

"At times, a Krishna Dvaipayana is born to a Shantanu as well. You were only a medium, mother. Bhishma would any way have renounced the kingdom. Your guilt has consumed you so far, mother! Bhishma was never responsible for that."

"I don't believe, son. Is a man capable of such a sacrifice?"

"The wise are capable of that, mother! ... Anyway, were you happy at your Baba's place before your marriage, bereft of any comforts?"

"Yes, my son!"

"And, now, when you have all the comforts of the world, all the luxuries, are you still happy?"

"I think I have never been happy at Hastinapur, not even for a day!"

"Thus you must conclude that happiness does not lie in wealth, power and might."

"How can I become happy, then?"

"You would have been happy at Parashara's cottage rather than coming down to this place," Vyasa smiled. "Come with me, away from this excitement and relax your agitated mind."

"I can't now, my son. I can't leave all this. I have these liabilities. Who do I entrust them with?"

"Bhishma."

"If I had to do that, why should I have taken the kingdom away from him in the first place?"

"Then the time to snap your attachment has still not arrived, mother! You must suffer some more."

"I talk not of bonds but of happiness!"

"One who is bound can never be happy, mother!

"Don't curse your mother, son."

"It is not a curse. I state a fact."

35

Ambika was in an awful state of both body and mind. She decided to resign herself to her fate. Anyway, things were not in her hands. Nothing went the way she would have liked to. She was abducted by Bhishma and handed over to Vichitravirya as a lifeless thing. But she could not consider herself an inanimate object.

She was now prone to constant ruminating. Her thoughts drifted like stray clouds blown away by strong winds in the sky. She thought about herself as a woman. Were women meant to be frail? But Amba, also, a woman, had never surrendered or submitted to others' will. Moreover, all men were not successful; even Bhishma, a paragon of might, had submitted himself to the domineering Satyavati, whom Ambika had come to know better after her encounter with her illicit son, Vedvyasa.

Wasn't even Satyavati a hapless woman plucked off her lover's embrace? Or had she, blinded by the glare of regality, abandoned her natural lover?

More than Satyavati, Ambika held Bhishma responsible for her misery. Why was Bhishma obsessed with arranging suitable women for others? Why should he have bothered himself to procure wives for the likes of Shantanu and Vichitravirya? Many men in this world stayed bachelor; many were not lucky enough to get a compatible spouse. That was not such a big deal. At least, Bhishma should not have put the princesses of Kashi in the miserable plight he had. Why should the three sisters have been made to pay the price of Bhishma's vow?

It was disgusting. Disgraceful. Why was she forced to comply with Satyavati's decree to produce an heir to the throne of Hastinapur and to submit herself to a strange despicable man? Was Ambika not a living being but a lump of feminine flesh? Was she an object, a means to realise another's wish.

To hell with that niyoga!

Ambika longed for no man, whether young, handsome, healthy or robust. All she desired was to be let alone in some secluded spot or given the right to die.

The niyoga was of course a well thought-out practice devised by the great sages. But it would have been welcome if Ambika had opted for it in earnest as a means to produce a son to provide her widowed self a support for the old age. But what she had to go through was revolting and outrageous. It was the rape of a woman against her will, ordained by her mother-in-law. No, she would not have that son!

Ambika retched. She wanted to throw up. She leaned over a pot kept beside her bed for the purpose. But nothing came out. Her sister Ambalika held her by the shoulders and tried to comfort her.

The physician was called. Surprised that his potions had not worked, he produced a fresh concoction. But Ambika threw it down the window.

Ambika's condition alarmed Ambalika who apprehended something uncanny coming her way.

She revealed her fears to Ambika, who consoled her: "Don't you worry. If anything unendurable happens to us, we will die."

"No! I feel they will not even let me die. I feel I will catch some crippling disease that will confine me to bed. It will be a life of torture and humiliation. Or I will be driven out of the royal palace and will roam the streets begging alms, without any abode or clothes or food. I am so afraid. How will I endure all that?"

"Nothing will happen to you. Do not forget we are the princesses of Kashi, queen consorts of Hastinapur. Bhishma is our custodian. And why should you panic, Ambalika? I am here to protect you," Ambika tried to console Ambalika.

But Ambalika was not to be reassured."I fear you too will abandon me the way Amba forsook us. Why do I feel that I will be apprehended by some wicked people who will thrash me so severely that my flesh will fly about in tiny pieces like beaten cotton, my bones will be broken and hurt beyond endurance, my body will be tossed into a raging fire and burnt like a piece of dry wood and my flesh will burn and I will suffer extreme pain?"

"What will you do then, Ambalika, when you will be subjected to such pain?" Ambika was solemn this time.

"I think I will embrace death."

"You are right! Death is the worst that can happen to one. Believe that there is God and have faith in him. He is a great judge. He can put everything right. Death is the ultimate solution he has offered in this world. When everything gets out of hand, death is available," Ambika put across her view.

"I agree, elder sister! But then I fear death as well. I think what will happen to me if I die and I tremble in fright," Ambalika's voice was faint, and she went pale.

Ambika discerned her younger sister's fright. She sent her to rest.

As for herself, Ambika felt absolutely relieved and content after she had got rid of that obnoxious potion prescribed by the state physician. There was no anxiety and no stress now.

36

Ambika was content because she thought that by throwing away medicines and skipping meals she would be able to kill herself and the little brute growing inside her womb. She was reduced to her own shadow, a spectre, a mere skeleton so much so that everyone from the nurses to the state physician was alarmed how she would deliver the baby. They perceived an imminent threat to the mother and the child. But that was not to be; the child fed on her entrails.

Whatever her presentiments and pangs during the pregnancy, whatever her travails, all were forgotten the moment she held the newborn. Defying all fears and speculation, it was a comely baby boy, alive and kicking.

Unlike Dvaipayana, the boy was fair in complexion, though his large dreamy eyes reminded one of his father. Satyavati was captivated by the long-awaited sight. She thought he was the one who would uphold the 'rashtra' (the nation) and hence called him Dhritrashtra.

The joy the child's birth brought to everyone was, though, short-lived. Shortly was it detected that the child was, his large beautiful eyes not-withstanding, sightless! Like a peacock's plume!

Shocked Ambika shut her eyes and lowered her head. "This was just inevitable to me," she gasped.

Satyavati was furious. She chided the rajavaidya (the state physician) who had first broken the news. How could he dare! He should have mulled over the news a thousand times before pronouncing it. He must be aware that if his words were proven wrong, he would be beheaded instantly.

The physician, however, stood by what he had diagnosed. He said, "I am helpless, queen mother! This is God's creation. It runs by his will. I can only suggest that it is due to some nutritional deficiency in the mother's diet."

Satyavati's rage was diverted to Ambika who she held primarily guilty for the mishap. The outburst was torrential: "This wretched woman, she never wanted to let me have a healthy and strong grandson. She fasted deliberately to deprive the babe in her womb of essential nutrition. She wept all along so that the child would be born blind. She forgot that the child was not only my grandson but also her son, whose kingship was going to make her the queen mother in future. She is surely an ill-fated women; otherwise why was she widowed! The wicked one first consumed her husband, and now she robs her son of his eyesight!"

And then her salvo was turned to Bhishma: "And then there is this Bhishma who abducted these wretched princesses. One of them ran away before marriage. The other two were widowed and now the son! Was there no other royal family or princess, in this world that he had to get these three?"

Satyavati targeted all. Only Dvaipayana Vyasa was spared; after all he was her own son.

When her steam was all spent, Satyavati sat down and wept bitterly.

Eventually, when she calmed down, Satyavati resumed her thinking. She must have a grandson. The first being born blind, let Ambika produce another one. After one child, a woman did not go barren; instead she is assured of her fecundity. And the first child being born blind did not mean that every other child would follow suit.

However, she realised Ambika would not conceive soon as she had just delivered a child. Moreover, she was not in good health. Why should Ambalika not produce the king of Hastinapur! Though senior, Ambika had marred her own chance by being callous.

She summoned Ambalika. It was a ruler's command-blunt and without a slightest hint of affection, the breach of which would fetch punishment.

Satyavati was straightforward with Ambalika. She told her in plain terms that she wanted a grandson to rule the kingdom of Hastinapur and Ambalika would have to produce that boy. And that grandson would be born through the appointed one of Satyavati's choice. Satyavati even disclosed the identity of the man-Davaipayana Vyasa-and the rituals to be observed.

Ambalika was secure as long as she was not menstruating. Ironically though, the queen mother's command so frightened her that the menstrual flow appeared at once. She hid nothing and Satyavati lost no time in rushing the horsemen off to fetch Vedvyasa.

The arrival of Vedvyasa paralysed Ambalika who had never anticipated such a hideous character in her bed chamber. She was horrified. She went pale. She had no strength left to get up and greet the great sage. Did she lie down unmoved or she swooned, she did not know!

37

The boy born to Ambalika was handsome but pale. Satyavati grumbled to Ambika: "The boy is weak. His colour is yellow. Who knows if he will survive and for how long? The rajavaidya says he is anaemic, which explains his paleness."

When Satyavati asked Ambika who between Dhritrashtra or Pandu should be the crown prince, Ambika refused to name a choice and left the matter to the queen mother's discretion.

Satyavati was incensed. "I least bother about what you wish. I am talking about the two children's imperfection. Dhritrashtra is born blind and Pandu is sick. Neither of them is fit or competent to be declared the crown prince. The Kuru empire stands where it was before these two were born."

Satyavati's wrath was against the two sisters Ambika and Ambalika who she deemed hostile to the Kuru family in that they had advertently ignored the physician's advice to be mindful of their diet.

"Give me a healthy grandson," she told Ambika in a rather subdued voice.

"Why, again?"

"Yes! Again," emphasised Satyavati.

To which Ambika offered no resistance.

Though Ambika had qualms about having brought forth a blind boy and had often felt sorry for her son, she did not think it was really her own fault. Was it none of the physician's, Vyasa's, queen mother's, the Creator's fault? If Ambika's will were supreme, would there be any niyoga to start with?

Now, another command!

Another niyoga!

Was it Ambika's will too? Suddenly a suppressed desire welled up within her. What if the queen mother appointed Bhishma this time? But that was a sheer wishful thinking, Ambika admitted.

Ambika thought of discussing it over with Ambalika but decided against it as she was too tender and timid. She might possibly not endure the weight of confidentiality and could spill out the whole thing.

Ambika's quest for an authentic confidant ended in her own chamber!

"Maryada! You are not married?" Ambika asked in an attempt to open up to her handmaid.

"No, my mistress!" said Maryada, who was obviously astonished at being called by her first name. And the mistress seemed overly curious about her personal life! Why?

"Why do you ask that?"

"Suppose you were shifted to nightly attendance, would that cause you much discomfort, Maryada?" asked Ambika.

"Not at all, my mistress! It will be an honour to me as otherwise I stay alone at my cottage. Here I will be enjoying your company, away from the horrors of loneliness and lechers."

"Then, I will direct your in-charge, who will give you a permanent posting here."

"So kind of you," Maryada clasped her hands in thankfulness.

What transpired between Ambika and Maryada was at once baffling and bewildering.

When Maryada reported for her nightly services, she detected a bedding conspicuously laid at the floor beside her mistress' regular bed. And, more stunningly, it was meant for her. She was to pass her night there beside her mistress.

As night progressed, the boundaries of class between the two ladies were broken down and they emerged as two friends willing to stand by each other in distress.

During their conversation, Ambika reminded Maryada of her beauty and youth and the ephemerality of beauty and youth. She convinced her that her beauty and youth were very much needed by her new bound sakhi.

"To be precise," said Ambika, "the mother queen requires a grandson to be seated upon the throne of Hastinapur."

"She has two," reminded Maryada.

"One is born blind and the other is sick. She wants a robust, healthy and capable grandson not invalid ones. Like the existing two grandsons, the third one too will be born by niyoga. The man appointed for this purpose is Vedvyasa, the great sage, but as a man he does not appeal to me. Actually, no other man does either. I want..."

"Yes, you want... What do you want, hon'ble queen?"

"I want you to take my place in the bed with Vedvyasa."

Maryada was surprised to hear this proposal.

"Excuse me, hon'ble queen! But do you think we will be able to guard this secret?"

"It will be so, Maryada, till this scheme lasts. No secrecy will be warranted after that."

"How will it benefit anyone? The great sage Vedvyasa is no mean drunkard that he will not be able to distinguish between Queen Ambika and maid Maryada. He will surely find out who shared his bed . And, the queen mother will be informed ..."

"That's exactly what I want, my young lady," Ambika

interrupted her. "I want you to please the great sage with your youth, beauty and servitude and want him to recognise you. I want the queen mother to realise that Ambika does not endorse her schemes and that the mother of her grandson is the maid Maryada."

Maryada still feared that the disclosure of the secret would be disastrous for the maid and her son, that they would be either imprisoned or exiled. "And you will still have to present yourself for the niyoga," she apprehended.

To allay her apprehensions, Ambika said, "that will not be. You and your child are safe because the queen mother will guard Vedvyasa's child and its mother at any cost. Mind that Vedvyasa is not simply a man appointed to perform this particular task. He is the queen mother's illicit son and, thus, his son from a maid will also be her own grandson."

"Is it true?" Maryada asked in disbelief.

"Absolutely true. And a highly guarded secret too. Now do you agree to defend me as you promised?

"I do. And I see the scheme will redeem us both."

Ambika was grateful. Clearly gratified.

38

Vedvyasa could not dishonour his mother's bidding. He was physically there but his mind was withdrawn. What was the meaning of niyoga? Wasn't it imperative for the woman to be religiously inclined to procreate?

On the last two occasions, Vedvyasa had noticed the reluctance of both Ambika and Ambalika. Were they not willing to have a child or was Dvaipayana not likeable to them as the appointed one? In the first case, it was an atrocity; and in the second case, niyoga amounted to fornication.

Still he was there on his mother's command, which he must yield to.

Anyway, he was there not to solicit sensual pleasure or earn a beautiful damsel's praise. He was guided by an ethical obligation.

In the room, dimly lit by a solitary lamp, Vedvyasa was greeted by Ambika, who was mysteriously veiled, perhaps so instructed by the queen mother.

Scrupulously, Vedvyasa quizzed the woman in the veil.

"Why this veil, my lady?"

"To gain your favour, O Noble One!"

"What has a favour to do with the veil? Who are you?"

"A maid."

"Your name?"

"Maryada!"

"Ambika has directed you to be here?"

"Yes, Noble One!"

"Why?"

"She could not accept niyoga."

"Why should she.send you?"

"Out of fear!"

"Who was she afraid of?"

"The queen mother."

Vedvyasa contemplated the intricacy of the situation. He realised that Ambika and Ambalika had previously acted under compulsion. And now Ambika had come up with this device.

He stood up. "You are free, Maryada," he said. "You are under no obligation to produce a child for your queen Ambika."

Maryada was put off. She was under no compulsion. Her desire for a child was her sole motive.

Vedvyasa understood. He could not ethically deny Maryada her request. He could not discriminate in the matter of a maternal desire. He could not ridicule penury that way.

"Your wish will be fulfilled, young lady," he declared. "You will bear a boy, who will be a brother to Dhritarashtra and Pandu through me. Being the mother of the princes' brother, you will not be a maid anymore."

Maryada kneeled before him in veneration.

Satyavati was thoroughly upset, intensely shaken.

Her proposal to prepare Ambalika again for niyoga was rejected outright by Vedvyasa, who contended, "There is a limit to niyoga. mother! If I produce more than three children for the Kuru dynasty, I will not be considered an 'appointed man', but an adulterer ... Now you have three grandsons. The third one is due to be brought forth by Maryada."

Convincing Satyavati was a near impossible task. "Maryada is a maid. She is not Vichitravirya's field. Her son could neither be a prince nor my grandson," she announced and then relented, "But, of course, for he is your son, I will take utmost care so that he will not suffer. Being your son's mother, Maryada will not remain a maid. But she can neither be a queen nor my daughter-in-law!'

"As you wish, mother!"

Those were Vedvyasa's parting words to Satyavati, who was left there in a whirlpool of thoughts. Should she leave it to Bhishma to decide?

39

Bhishma looked out of the window where, in the garden, the children indulged in frolicking sport. They were five in all: Dhritarashtra, Pandu, Vidur, Krip, and Kripi. The eldest of them was Krip, and Kripi was his twin sister; Shantanu, in his last days, had brought them here after taking permission of their father, the sage Sharadvan. Younger to them was twelve-year-old Dhritarashtra while Pandu was about eleven and Vidur ten.

The children were confined to the place for significant reasons. Dhritarashtra was visually impaired, Pandu was physically invalid and Vidur was a bookworm. Pandu was simple at heart and self-mortifying and not the least crafty and shrewd like Dhritrashtra. Vidur was apt to put puzzles about dharma, the ethics, the creation, God, the society, the state, the king, and the like.

As his roving eyes focussed on Kripi, Bhishma, reminded of her age, thought that he must find a suitable match for her. It amused him to think that he was father to those kids. How ironical! How he had resolved to stay away from the botherations of the household and how events had amassed a varied group of people around him-Satyavati, Ambika, Ambalika, Maryada, Dhritrashtra, Pandu, Vidur, Krip and Kripi-for whom he had to fend. He must arrange wealth, servants, teachers, soldiers, cowshed, stable, everything. But whose was that all? Not Bhishma's of course. He was simply a guardian. All that belonged to the future crown prince. But who? Their biological father had spared not a moment in pronouncing his verdict.

Dvaipayana had minced no words in declaring that all were equal to him. The sun, the wind and mother Ganga held no distinction while showering their blessing. So did Dvaipayana treat Dhritrashtra, Pandu and Vidur as equal. Now it was up to Bhishma to judge who should inherit the kingdom of Hastinapur - a very difficult task.

Though Dhritrashtra, the eldest, was the most rightful one, he was blind. It would be unjust to thrust the kingly duties upon him. And no less unjustified would it be to Pandu and Vidur, the two-eyed ones, who would be forced to cater to the whims and wishes of an individual physically less equipped than them.

Where was the option?

Bhishma looked skywards: What a moment of history, this, O God! What was in store for the subjects of a kingdom kept deprived of a competent ruler?

40

Bhishma trained the princes in hunting, which was easily the most common form of exercise in arms and physical training.

When Vidur came back from such a week-long outing in the surrounding forests of Hastinapur, his mother asked him how he liked it .

"Nothing likeable in that, mother," Vidur complained. "To kill harmless animals in their abodes! I just don't appreciate this game of the Kshatriyas! What is so gallant about that?... Watching the sightless Dhritrashtra simulating solemn concentration while shooting aimlessly into the space amuses me, mother. And when an attendant presents some animal killed by someone else at his feet with words of compliment for his hunting skill, it infuriates me!"

Maryada smiled, "You must cajole the sightless prince, my son, or his heart will break. He is already so distressed."

Vidur's responses were generically like his ascetic father's. His pleas inspired awe in his mother, who stared at him stupefied. "Killing is not a kshatriya's resolve," he said, "justice is. It is to affirm justice that violence is resorted to. Regrettably, justice has now evaporated out of the kshatriyas' violence. The indulgence of hunting was allowed to them in order to maintain their imperial passion. Now that is reduced to stark enjoyment, which is but a sham."

Maryada was overwhelmed. Such wisdom! Why, he

was mere sixteen. He was overgrowing his mother in intellect and in person. Even his experiences exceeded his mother's. And the gap was to consistently increase. Maryada was overwhelmed with gratitude, to God, and also to the great sage who ignored her lowly status to bless her with a son, such a son! And to Bhishma who never discriminated against her son. And to Queen Ambika who had been instrumental in letting that occasion into her life, into the life of her humble maid whom she regarded as her mate.

Vidur complained against Dhritrashtra, who was prone to exploiting his blindness to his advantage, that he was being unfair to Pandu who was by all measures superior to him in archery. Vidur even accentuated his aloofness in those matters.

"Do you ever crave equality with the princes, my son?" Maryada said.

"No, mother, I rather congratulate myself for not being a prince, otherwise I would have been drawn into unreasonable blood-shed, would have been supporting the unjust out of selfishness, and would have been loving hypocrisy more than truth. Craving, possessiveness, competition-these are not the ornaments of humanity, mother! These do not liberate man or elevate man! They cause but degeneration, nothing else."

And regarding Bhishma, he said, "I see no fault in him. He is a sublime image of human attributes. But, mother, I fear he may yield to Dhritrashtra's sinful demands like he did with the grandmother's insatiable desires."

Suspicious and scared, Maryada looked at him and hugged him, "you are right, my son!"

Ambalika was engaged with her son, Pandu, who betrayed signs of peevishness, which was unusual for one so young. "Hunting is supposed to elevate one's spirits," she contended. She wanted to know the reason why Pandu was cross. It was the same-Dhritrashtra; he exploited every situation to cash in on his blindness. And, ironically, Pandu was having to pay the price of his own sightedness.

Pandu described a recent incident in which Dhritrashtra had claimed two deer killed by him. Why? "Because I loved him; and because he loved me! How clever!"

"There is only one way to reconcile with him," grumbled Pandu. "Give him what is his, and also give him what is not his."

"Oh! why God." Ambalika felt giddy.

Dhritrashtra, as he was relaxing after hunting, was asked by Ambika: "You didn't cause inconvenience to them at hunting?"

Dhritrashtra's harsh and adversarial face quickly assumed the expression of weak innocence. He simulated a sweet softness in his speech. "Mother, how could I, born-blind, bother them? In fact, they bother me! Is it reasonable to take a sightless one to hunting? But they do as they wish?"

Ambika was by then accustomed to her son's melodramatic outbursts. She knew that her son, who was increasingly an alien to her for those very reasons, though blind to his outer world, had created a starkly different world in the dark depths of his bosom. Ambika was ever outraged by her son's dubious attempts to con her. In those moments, he looked not her own son but Satyavati's grandson instead.

She reprimanded him for being melodramatic again and gave her a lesson or two in how to behave with his brothers, even as she pitied him for not admitting his mistakes. Through the discourse Dhritrashtra persisted in his plea that actually it was he who was wronged.

When Ambika stated that Bhishma's presence at the game ruled out any injustice, Dhritrashtra became infuriated. He accused Bhishma of gross felony in that he had gifted over to Pandu the kingdom that actually was to be inherited by him being the elder son of King Vichitravirya.

Ambika was stunned. "Nature has pledged that you will not rule," she reacted angrily. "Had it willed you to rule, it would not deny you the sight."

"It was not God who did it to me."

"Then, who did it-me?"

"Yes, you. The grandma has told me all; you never wanted me to be born. You kept yourself starved and in suffering, so that I was blinded. You wanted me to die, but God willed otherwise. In spite of you, I survived, mother! And ... And ..."

"And what?"

"And you will see. Despite you, aunt Ambalika, Pandu and Bhishma himself, I will rule over Hastinapur. No one will be able to stop me."

"My conscience is right in dictating that you are not my son but your grandma's grandson."

"Of course! I'm her grandson; I feel more pride in being her grandson than your son. A boatman's daughter, she now sits pretty as the queen mother, whereas you, a king's daughter, is reduced to the status of a prisoner-an ordinary maid. I regret being your son."

And he stood up, picked his stick and walked out.

Recovering from a brief stupor, Ambika resolved never to emulate Satyavati. She would tread her own path and stick to that, come what may.

41

Bhishma had believed that once Pandu was coronated, he would be absolved of all liabilities and free to lead a life of his own. That was, however, easier said than done.

When he begged mother Satyavati's leave from Hastinapur, presumably into renunciation, she brushed off the very idea downright.

"Bhishma, my son!" she laughed. "Go to every household in Hastinapur and ask every child. Then, you will know you are already a renouncer. Being in the royal palace, you have abandoned all pleasures, all enjoyment. You sleep on the floor and eat food fit only for a recluse. You crave nothing, neither kingdom nor splendour. Your sole engagement is meditation. If that is not renouncing, what is?"

Bhishma was halted in his track.

"Dhritrashtra is born-blind. Vidur is a book-worm. As for Pandu, he is too feeble to even withstand a breeze. I have witnessedthe enthronement of Chitrangada and Vichitravirya. What was their fate? One was killed by the enemy and the other one by disease. Do you think Pandu is capable of resisting the onslaught of malicious kings, the conspiracies of the Kuru chieftains and deadly diseases?"

Bhishma concluded that his moment of liberation had not yet arrived.

Once when Bhishma was resting in his portion of the palace Ambika visited him. Though surprised and concerned, his worries were allayed by a pleasing smile on her face.

What unfolded through her ensuing submission was, however, not palatable to Bhishma.

It was essentially about Dhritrashtra.

"Dhritrashtra is my son but he is not under my control," she moaned. "I have utterly failed to regulate his thought or conduct... He says he is no Bhishma. That he has not abstained from kingdom or woman. He complains that though his kingdom was wrongfully snatched away from him and bestowed on Pandu, he will not sit quietly if he is not even married."

"Who prevents him?"

"None. But he is aware that no girl will ever opt for him at a swayamvara. No gentleman in his senses will ever think of marrying his daughter to one born blind. And he lacks the strength to abduct a girl. There is only one competent man who can accomplish it for him-you! You have done it in the past. First, you provided a young wife to an old man. Then you were assigned to arrange wives for an impotent diseased youth. On this occasion, you have to arrange a wife for a blind and pervert prince ...but please ensure that no girl is unwillingly forced into Dhritrashtra's arms."

Bhishma promised: "No girl will be abducted now for providing a wife to either Dhritrashtra, Pandu or Vidur."

Ambika left, gratified.

Among the match proposed for Dhritrashtra and Pandu, Bhishma short-listed the Gandhara king Subal's daughter, Gandhari, Kuntibhoja's foster daughter, Pritha, and the Bhadra King Shalya's younger sister, Madri. King Devak's daughter Paransavi, born of a maid, could be considered, with Devak's consent, for Vidur who, himself a maid's son, would not be eligible for a princess.

Bhishma took it upon himself to procure, through the proper process, Gandhari for Dhritrashtra, Madri for Pandu, and Panasavi for Vidur.

42

Subal, the king of Gandhara, Prince Shakuni, and Kanik, the Minister of Hastinapur, sat in a huddle at a private chamber in the royal palace of Gandhara.

Subal was offended that he was expected to endorse his daughter's marriage to the blind Dhritrashtra. "If the proposal were for Pandu, I would have felt somewhat honoured. But Dhritrashtra..." he said to Kanik.

"Gandhararaja!" Kanik spoke out softly. "You must be aware thatmatrimonial matches in royal families are governed by political prospects rather than personal preferences. Marriages are in principle a union of political entities. Have you any friends in your neighbourhood?"

"No, none."

"That's it! Suppose there were an aggression against your kingdom. Would you be able to defend yourself? Do you have a strong army?"

"No! The Gandharas do not make able soldiers."

"Why don't you induct soldiers then from other states?"

"I don't have enough funds to pay for them."

"That's why! It would be strategically wise to gain the support of a worthy friend. Forge relations with Hastinapur by accepting their proposal. That would bring an end to many of your problems. We would extend to you all kind of support."

"Should I enjoy that comfort even when my daughter

goes through the ordeal of marrying someone born blind?"

"O King of Gandhara! In Hastinapur, Gandhari would not be put to any ordeal. She will rule there as a queen, all heavenly pleasures will be hers."

"Will that compensate for the want of a capable husband?"

"Dhritrashtra is a good-looking prince. The sightlessness does not make a man impotent. He may not be blessed with working eyes, but there are a lot others to look on his behalf ... And even if you rebuff us and decline to marry Gandhari to Dhritrashtra, how will you protect her against others who might not be as respectable? Suppose they abduct her. How will you ensure a respectful and comfortable future for your daughter? Remember Bhishma? Abduction is the kshatriyas' prime right."

As Kanik proceeded with his pleas, terror seized Subal and Shakuni who sought some time to consider it over.

In the evening, Kanik was invited to the palace by Subal, who eventually conceded to his demands with certain riders.

On Subal's insistence, it was decided that the marriage ceremony would be held at Hastinapur and not Purushpur. And Shakuni would accompany Gandhari to Hastinapur and stay there as an honourable member of the Kaurava council.

His demands granted, the king of Gandhara consented to dispatch Gandhari and Shakuni at the earliest auspicious moment to Hastinapur.

43

It had been a tedious travel for Shakuni. From Gandhara to Hastinapur was a remarkable change of terrain. Everything was changed, from topography to human figure, their appearance, language, and conduct. He had been preoccupied with strange thoughts. Even Gandhari had been unusually reticent all the while. Few words were exchanged between them for all his conscious efforts.

He remembered his father's departing words at Gandhara: "Son! I will recognise you as Shakuni when you will convert Gandhari's present defeat into a noose against the Kauravas. Maybe this moment of vanquishment has visited us so that the Gandharas will attain enhancement. You must work towards that. The more you advance into the Kurus' field of governance, the more gratified I will be."

Shakuni was not aware if their father had briefed Gandhari separately. What if she assumed that she was thrust into this quagmire in order to serve their own selfish ends or to forestall any debacle that might ruin them otherwise? Wouldn't her wrath turn on the Gandharas as well?"

Gandhari was supported by the maids Kesari and Vasanti down the royal chariot. Satyavati rushed forward to embrace her and she held her at arms' length and lifted her veil.

Lo! She had a band tied on her eyes!

"O Noble Grandmother," she explained. "A woman whose husband is endowed with inner eyes (sightless) has no right to use her normal eyes."

Satyavati was baffled.

"I thought you will be a support to Dhritrashtra. He would see through your eyes."

"A pious woman would never compete with her husband in any sphere, Grandmother!" Gandhari was quick to remark.

Satyavati studied the woman who stood so calm and unruffled before her. A fair, tall and strong lady in her teens, Gandhari looked gorgeous. She had assets to disarm any man. Besides youth and charm, she possessed strong-mindedness as an added attribute.

Satyavati revisited her perception of Gandhari when left to herself at the end of the day that was mostly devoted to accommodating her new guests.

She ruminated over the day's events and thought about Gandhari: How fair she was like a chunk of churned cream that would be soiled by a mere touch of hand! So tall, like a pine tree. A sharp nose, a prominent chin. The luxuriant hair that would change their hue with the beams of sunshine. Only if she could have her band removed to have a look at her eyes! She was told that the colour of the Gandhara damsel's eyes was either blue or green.

Satyavati felt checkmated by Gandhari's move in which she sensed a dreadful design. Why she had blindfolded herself ahead of her arrival in Hastinapur? She chose not to witness the Kauravas' magnificence. She chose to obscure Satyavati's beauty and authority. She ignored even Bhishma's dignity.

She was apprehensive of Gandhari's intention. Personally, Satyavati was least perturbed by who would occupy the throne of Hastinapur-Pandu or Dhritrashtra. Both were her grandsons. But that ambitious woman Gandhari with that blindfold scared her. Who could tell what lurked behind that band on her eyes! Was it to ignore the Kurus? Was she protesting her marriage to a blind man? Or she wanted to imply that she did not care for the Kurus or did not even fear them?

Was she going to prove a thorn in her flesh, Satyavati shuddered.

44

The night next to the nuptials, Dhritrashtra was eventually closeted with Gandhari. To start with, he said to her: "Why this, O damsel of Gandhara! Why should you blindfold yourself for my sake?"

Gandhari managed a smile, though she knew her smile was out of place. Dhritrashtra might be designated 'prajna chakshu' (the one with inner eyes), but to recognise a smile on a woman's face a man must use his eyes. Howsoever sensitive Dhritrashtra's palms may be, they would not acknowledge the smile on Gandhari's cheeks. Only his ears could tell him whether she was smiling or crying.

"The one for whom I willingly fettered my feet, for whose sake I wore bracelets on my wrists, what great accomplishment is this to put this band on my eyes!" she said.

"Fairly witty, Gandhari," Dhritrashtra admired her. "But such a sacrifice for a total stranger!"

"This is not sacrifice but recognition, O Noble One!"

"Recognition? What recognition?"

"The recognition of yourself! Of your personality! Of your strengths and limitations."

Dhritrashtra paused a moment before resuming: "You are right, sweetheart! They fear me and avoid calling me blind and therefore they use a euphemism 'prajna chakshu.' In fact, you are the one endowed with the inner eyes."

"How, O Noble One?"

"When you learnt about my blindness you knew how jealous a blind man is and presumed how I would react to your rejection or consent. And hence you tied a band on your eyes on the way before having to look at me."

"I don't believe you are that jealous. Otherwise, you would not keep quiet upon your kingdom being bestowed on your younger brother."

"Oh no! Not so loud," Dhritrashtra was hit on the vulnerable side. "You are not aware. They are all against me-Grandma Satyavati, the Sire Bhishma, Pandu, Vidura, and even my mother Ambika. They all favour Pandu-the ministers, the Kuru chiefs, and soldiers. I am all alone here."

"Not now. No more. We are one-you and me. With me is Shakuni, our father the king of Gandhara, the kingdom of Gandhara." Gandhari solaced him. "We are all yours. Say are you alone?"

"O my dear!" Dhritrashtra was rejuvenated. "You are not only my passion but my strength as well. In a moment, you make me Kama, the god of love, and Mahadeva, the destroyer of Kama."

Dhritrashtra embraced Gandhari, who offered no resistance. She said, "O Noble One! This kingdom is yours and will remain yours."

"The state of Hastinapur would not recognise the verdict that a prince born blind cannot occupy the throne."

"Rightly said! But anyone else doing so would only act like his deputy like Bhishma did."

"You puzzle me, Gandhari!"

"It simply implies that the day the elder prince's son is born he will be declared the crown prince."

"Gandhari!"

"Yes, O Noble One! You should talk to the Sire and the Grandma. And I promise I will get you a son before a son is born to Pandu."

It was a new birth for Dhritrashtra, who saw his

fortune rising on the horizon. Gandhari was not his spouse; she was the harbinger of good luck. He, who had felt so lonesome, vulnerable and helpless, now experienced a surge of zeal and weal in his blood.

"You give me so much," Dhritrashtra was overwhelmingly obliged. "Ask me whatever you will."

Gandhari laughed, "O Noble One! What do you have now that is not mine?"

Dhritrashtra was again outwitted.

"Nothing," he said.

"I knew that," Gandhari quipped. "You want to gift me something out of my own wealth. You are very clever indeed. Honestly, I need nothing once I have got you."

She desired to visit her home with him but also contended that would not be feasible given his condition.

"You will go alone then?" The thought of departure on the very first night of union peeved him.

"I can but I won't. It would be disgraceful for a woman to go to her parents without her new-found partner."

"Why don't you call them here? And Shakuni can stay back with you... No, not at all indecent, a brother staying with his sister as her dependent. Moreover, he is younger than you. That should pose no problem. He will be inducted as an honourable member of the state council. I hope it is settled now!" Dhritrashtra would not let her go.

"How nice of you!" Gandhari said and stretched out easefully.

45

Kunti was no less terrified than depressed. A burden weighed heavily on her mind and on her breast.

Her maids and personal lady attendants appeared every other moment and teased her in glee and broke some fresh news.

There was hectic excitement all around. The palace of King Kuntibhoja had come live. It was the same palace that stood in full gloom here before. The father-daughter duo-Kuntibhoja and Kunti-passed days together without having a soul to speak to. There was none else in the family. Relations were few. Even her real father Shursena and brother Vasudeva had not visited the place even once; perhaps they did not want to her to rekindle her love for them once they had willingly offered their Pritha to King Kuntibhoja. Durvasa had been a rare guest.

Durvasa's visit was painfully alive in her heart. Even her father Kuntibhoja had warned her not to disclose it to anyone. Not only her father's honour but the whole family's honour was at stake. Had she committed such a great sin?

Now, on this day, as her maids and friends unfolded the list of the swayamvara contestants and informed her of each new arrival, she felt even more nervous, even more compunctious. Now she would be selecting a man of her liking as her life-partner. It was to be a union of mutual love and faith which she must honour at all costs. How could she afford to cheat him!

However, the issue was not confined to her own person. She was a part of a dynasty, the representative of a royal family. With her would be blemished all those who were related to her anyway. The more the intimate , the more they would be subjected to calumny. But what should she do with her deepening sense of sin?

Her steps towards the swayamvara pavilion were unsteady and slow. All eyes were set upon her. Some measured her and some tore her apart. The maids on her flanks held her as she mustered her strength and moved along.

Although Kuntibhoja's bard were singing praises of the family, Kunti felt as if someone was drumming into her ears or hammering a nail on her chest. Their exalting words uplifted the glory of the family whereas she sank lower in her self-esteem. Such was the family and such was she!

Why this swayamvara! Why did her father ever decide to hold such a ritual? Would she have declined the choice of her father? But she realised Kuntibhoja was obliged to do that. The fragrance of her beauty had transcended the boundaries of several kingdoms. Aryan warriors were like that. They swarmed wherever a battle, a gamble or a beautiful damsel was reported. Thus, Kuntibhoja opted for a swayamvara, ignoring how it would tax Kunti mentally.

"You have never been so shy," remarked her friend.

Kunti tripped. The friend had to hold her. In fact she has always been shy. It was so much due to her shyness, her inability to say 'no' that she was seduced into acting against her will. Her modesty had proved her bane.

She caught the applause of the bards. Now they were eulogising Pandu, the King of Hastinapur, a descendant of Bharata, Puru, Yayati, Shantanu and Bhishma. A vast and mighty empire that was renowned for righteousness, wealth and valour. She looked up. Pandu was eyeing her, trying to give a luring smile. Young and good-looking, he was noticeably pale! Do they have so much gold in Hastinapur that they turn pale, she was mused? Her mind raced. She thought about Vedvyasa and Bhishma, about Adhiratha, Hastinapur, the illegitimate sons, the Bharata dynasty.

She felt giddy. And before the bards would eulogise some other king or prince, she put the garland upon Pandu.

Kuntibhoja hugged her: "My dear daughter! You have fulfilled my hopes. I never thought of a groom better than the King of Hastinapur."

Kunti was overly happy. There were congratulations and jubilations all around. The contestants departed in succession.

She stood there wondering in awe.

46

Before arriving at Hastinapur, Kunti had witnessed the splendour of Mathura and Bhojpur, the citadel of the Yadavas, but this was a stunning revelation. Hastinapur was a stark emblem of splendour and magnificence. A rudimentary comparison brought forward the distinct vastness and sophistication of her new home. The influence of a luxurious way of living was writ large on the royal family. At Bhojpur, she treated her maid, her nurse as one of her family so very different here in Hastinapur! She heard about Bhishma who had given himself to austerity and reclusion despite his undisputed position as the patron and guardian of the royal clan.

A small tap at her door.

She looked up. It was Pandu. The maids left her and the door was shut from without.

Pandu sat down upon the bed beside her. He praised her beauty and hugged her. Her emotions, her limbs were stirred into a passionate embrace.

But! A huge but!

Pandu slackened his grip.

He was excited. He was eager. But he could not consummate.

Kunti took his inaction as modesty, which she appreciated at these initial hours. It was reasonable, she concluded. They must be familiar with each other first. For familiarity would breed intimacy, which would breed love, and love would ignite conjugation.

Kunti initiated: "My real name is Pritha, of course. I am called Kunti as the adopted daughter of Kuntibhoja. You may know that Shursena of Mathura was my father. He gave me over to his aunt's son, King Kuntibhoja, as the latter was childless."

"My father Shursena is no more," she continued in response to Pandu's question. "And you may have heard that my brother Vasudeva and sister-in-law Devaki are kept in prison by Kansa, who is defiant and would listen to no one, not even the council of the Yadavas. He is now a despot out to destroy the very governance system of the Yadavas."

"Why doesn't Kuntibhoja engage Kansa in battle?" Pandu said.

"Kansa enjoys the patronage of King Jarasandha of Magadha. If there is a battle, Yadavas on both sides will be killed. My brother Vasudeva..." Kunti broke into tears, which shattered Pandu's restraint. He could not resist the temptation offered by the situation.

A youthful, voluptuous Kunti was in his arms. He was shortly at the height of excitement that he feared would incinerate him-without Lord Mahadeva having to open his third eye.

Kunti was again misled by her innocence. She assumed Pandu was suffering in his attempt to restrain himself for her sake! She loved him even more for that.

In an effort to prolong the conversation, Pandu referred to sage Durvasa and his presence at her place.

Kunti was stung. Why Durvasa? Was he aware of what had transpired between the sage and her? Was he apprised of the banal episode somewhere during the long journey from Bhojpur to Hastinapur?

It was a fairly lengthy interrogation about Durvasa.

This alarmed Kunti: why should he ask all that?

"Why did he visit Bhojpur?" Pandu seemed adamant.

"He practised some system of meditation, some experiment, some new research in the sphere of knowledge."

"But he is considered to be very short-tempered."

"Which he is. Rather crazy," Kunti was getting to feel irritated, losing her patience.

"You must have served him well."

That was too much.

Kunti resorted to what could be a woman's last resort. She submitted her whole self to her man who braced for a passionate response, held her in a tightening embrace. But the next moment, agony was impressed on his face as he struggled against himself. He lost his grip. He panted. His face was warped.

"I don't feel fine," said he.

He got up and walked out.

Kunti sat on, dumbfounded.

Her misfortune was still a-haunting her, she thought. Her husband had somehow got the wind of that shady incident of her past. That was inevitable. One must pay for one's folly.

Her resentment against Pandu was immense. What right had he to persecute her like that! Was a slip committed in innocent ignorance so grave that one's whole life would be devastated? That was solely unreasonable. Would Kunti abandon him similarly if she got such an information about him?

Soon her reason got better of her wrath. What would she gain by resenting her husband? She should not emulate Ganga who deserted Shantanu. Where would she belong to besides Pandu? Back to Bhojpur to stigmatise Kuntibhoja? It was to save his honour that he had dispatched the newborn baby boy so far away. If she returned to Bhojpur, wouldn't she be smirching her father's repute? Then Mathura? But who was there to support her in that town? What comforts would she get in Kansa's regime?

It was a male-dominated society where men would have their way. If she antagonised her husband, she would have no place in her own home or in her parents. She must strike some compromise with her husband, and conform to his whims and fancies?

She brooded throughout that sleepless night. She was concerned about her future. What shape was her life going to take? What about her dreams that she had cherished as Kuntibhoja's daughter or after she had selected Pandu at the swayamvara, as the queen of Hastinapur? How short-lived was her dream that was shattered by King Pandu at a single stroke!

In a secluded chamber of his palace, Pandu lay straight on his back, tears in his eyes, staring blankly at the ceiling. This despondency was rare. Kunti was his wife, not a maid who could be brushed off at will. It was not a union for a few days. How long would he seek excuses to stay away from her? It would be better if he had pledged celibacy like the venerable Bhishma. But he would be facing a different ordeal here all his life, with Kunti sucking his blood for ever like Kritya the giantess.

However, he was definitely not like Bhishma; he knew he was weak in flesh. The mere sight of a feminine figure was enough to excite him. Either there should be no desire or there should be the required potency.

Pandu must do something about it. He should either seek the physicians' help or forge an equanimity, or shift to some faraway place, too far away from Kunti where there would be no one to test his potency.

Eventually, good sense prevailed.

As dawn descended, he took his decision. He would not, tormented by humiliation and Kunti's terrifying presence, hide from his subjects. He would go for a universal military exploit and establish new standards of the Bharata dynasty.

As the nascent beams of the rising sun kissed his palace, he went to sleep sufficiently relieved and relaxed.

Kunti woke up late. She felt heavy-hearted and her eyes burnt. She was still depressed and wary of the last night's events, which she believed would be replicated every night now. This was a period of transition. While the sages continued to uphold the sanctity, utility and sublimity of the Sanatana religion, the royalty was embracing change and setting new norms for itself and it was further divided on certain lines. The sages were selfless in their approach whereas the kings were propelled by self and pride. Consequently, the society was losing its generosity of vision and Kunti, a typically innocent adolescent girl, was being branded a sinner.

Men were naturally harsh and perhaps even ruthless. Even a humble man like Kuntibhoja had become merciless -and that too against a newborn child whom he ordered to be disposed of through a maid. Durvasa had asserted it was not a sin but Kunti believed that even if it was a sin by the changing standards of society, the sin must be attributed to the man. Why should Kunti bear the brunt?

She learnt through a maid that King Pandu was preparing to march for a universal military triumph. She was relieved.

"Maybe he has not disclosed my shady episode to anyone," said she to herself. "He knows it will not glorify him as a husband in any way. He has perhaps overlooked my guilt but decided to be away from Hastinapur for long under the pretext of this military exploit. There will be enough time in between when he may calm down or I may hit upon some way out of this labyrinth."

Satyavati lost no time in summoning Bhishma when she got the news.

Their discourse focussed on Pandu's prospective military march and how to prevent it.

Bhishma approached Pandu, who pretended to be

very busy, but he could not deceive Bhishma's inspecting eyes.

About his plans to march, Pandu said, "The kings around the arid areas of the Kuru region have become insurgents. They need to be disciplined."

Apparently convinced, Bhishma said, "I have full faith in you. But I have a submission. The Kuru dynasty is virtually barren. I want you to have many children. Another marriage will do the trick... I am going to beg Madrapati Shalya for his younger sister."

"How does it relate to my march?"

"It does. I am taking with me the minister Kanik, the priest Vasubhuti, several Brahmins and the four-winged army. Thusthe force left will be insufficient for your mission. So you may carry on with your preparations but you will not march until I return."

"I can see you have planned to stop me. But I am not retreating to the palace. I will stay at the military camp till your return and engage the men in military exercises."

"Agreed," said Bhishma as he prepared to leave.

47

"O Noble One!" Gandhari said, "I have heard that devar (husband's younger brother) is camping at the cantonment, leaving his bride behind at the palace."

"Yes, I have also heard that," responded Dhritrashtra.

"Why?"

"He intends to march on a digvijaya (universal conquest)."

"Who will hold the reigns of the kingdom in his absence?"

"Pitravya (uncle) Bhishma is there. He has been doing it on such occasions."

"Shakuni contends it was alright when you two brothers were young. Now as you have achieved adulthood and can take care of your liabilities, why bother him? In devar's absence, you should do that... Shakuni says you are the real master of the kingdom. Pandu was installed to assist you. It may be a bit cumbersome to you, but it will put you in consultation and contact with the ministers and the councillors. You may even appoint some ministers of your favour, so that they could speak for us when our son becomes eligible to rule."

"Will Pitravya Bhishma allow that?"

"Shakuni says the kingdom is not awarded but has to be acquired. Effort is the basic tenet of governance."

Gandhari waited for Dhritrashtra's response before resuming. "Is Kunti not beautiful? Is she not young?"

"I can't see for myself but I have heard that she is extremely beautiful and quite young, just twenty."

"Why then should devar leave her and go for his universal conquest? There must be something else behind his decision, I think."

"What?"

"Kunti has apparently failed to bind devar. Doesn't it please you?"

"Please me, why?"

"Kunti will not procreate a prince. Our son will be born first and we will try to have him declared the crown prince."

Dhritrashtra felt she was gripped by politics, Shakuni's brand of politics.

48

The young Madraraja Shalya received Bhishma personally and took him to his palace.

Due protocol was followed to accommodate the accompanying minister, priest and brahmins. The soldiers were camped at the cantonment.

Bhishma addressed Shalya, who was obviously curious about the unplanned visit: "O Madraraja! I am out to look for a second queen for my nephew and the king of Hastinapur, Pandu. I heard about your younger sister Madri. I am here to get her."

"You said 'a second queen,' which implies King Pandu is already married?"

"Yes, we follow polygamy in our clan."

"And polyandry too?"

"No, our clan is absolutely patriarchal. We don't observe polyandry."

"But, the Panchalas do. And the neighbours do influence us."

"Panchalas are, of course, our neighbours. But we have never been friendly with them."

Their discourse drifted to various systems of marriages.

"As a convention, we take a fee at the time of the 'kanyadan' (giving away a girl in marriage)," said Shalya.

"Not a good custom but we will give the fee," rejoined Bhishma.

A heated debate ensued over several such issues. They spoke on the merits and demerits of each of the contemporary customs regarding marriage.

"I am not aware of what prevailed in the matriarchal society but in the patriarchal set-up women and men do not enjoy equal rights." Shalya said, "And women are subordinate to men."

Bhishma thought to himself: This young man was unlike other kings. While the Aryavarta royalty was changing, here was an orthodox man, a relic of an era gone by. He did not harbour any inferiority complex.

Embroiled in the discussion with the king, Bhishma started doubting whether his own assumptions were weak.

He said: "Madraraja! Nature has ordained that a woman and a man born in separate hours are obliged to stay under one roof after marriage. One of them must leave home for the other. I think humans are engaged in various experiments and no single arrangement has withstood the test of time, none has proved to be perfect. Societies confined to a single village and that have no problems pertaining to the inheritance of personal property have a simple system: the newly-wed couples are given a separate new cottage apart from their respective homes. But in societies not confined to a village, like the royal kshatriya community, one party has to shift with the other. As kshatriyas own properties and wealth, inheritance is also a problem among them. Among us, a man's property is to be inherited by his son. Thus the bridegroom would not leave his place after the marriage, but the bride moves to his house."

"So far I do agree with you," said Shalya, "but I think the son is the real inheritor of his father's property. And the children are also the parents' property. Thus when a girl shifts to her father-in-law's house as a bride, it is virtually her father or brother's wealth that is thus transferred. Therefore, they must get the fee."

Bhishma was amused. She could be anyone's daughter, she could be anyone's bride, but it was the obligation of the society to ensure that no one was exploited, insecure or disgraced.

He said: "It cannot be easily or presently concluded which side of the argument, which of the customs is superior. We need to agree on the issue concerning the marriage of Pandu and Madri. What do you say?"

"I have already consented."

"And you need no further details?"

"It suffices me to know that King Kuntibhoja's daughter had willingly selected Pandu at the swayamvara which proves his worth and eligibility."

"So it's agreed?"

"Absolutely," declared Shalya.

And Bhishma ordered the minister to gift Shalya even more than he would expect.

"Give him much more than he expects as fee: that would suit his and our stature and repute."

The minister submitted that his orders would be obeyed to every detail.

49

Kunti all but cried.

What man she had chosen for her husband who, when annoyed, would not tell why. Did he really know about the dark chapter in her life? But how and when? Oh, that couldn't be. Otherwise he couldn't have pretended that he was enamoured of her.

Ironically, it was her own decision, her own choice and, hence, she was in no moral position to complain.

So was it beyond all hopes? Would Pandu never return to her? No! That couldn't be! Maybe he would be subdued during the intervening time. They might then come together, discuss the matter and reach some compromise. Then she would convince him that, good or bad, she was his wife. He could be pleased or displeasedwith her but the society would never sanction him to desert her. When Gautama had abandoned Ahilya, Rama and Vishvamitra had compelled him to take her back. A wife was the honour and dignity of her man. If she chose to desert her husband, who would defend the dignity of her man?

Why Madri? Pandu had got a second wife Madri. She was said to be very beautiful. He would live with her and they would enjoy life together. Kunti would be held not only guilty but also tainted. She cursed Pandu. If he intended to abandon her, he might but why tarnish her thus?

And her wrath was diverted to Bhishma! He was the

real culprit. He should have persuaded Pandu to compromise; instead he went off to find him another wife. He who was without a woman himself, he had taken it upon himself to locate women for others! Why didn't he interrogate Pandu about his march, so soon after he had got a wife? Why?

Then Kunti realised that her pride was going to do no good to her, fetch her no help! This society belonged to men only and only men could dominate in it. Only a man's ego would be appeased; only his comforts would be taken care of. If a man so willed it, he could lift the woman like a lifeless object and embrace her or he could cast her away and pick up another woman like a new plaything. This was proved by Durvasa, by her biological father Shursena, by her foster father Kuntibhoja and now by Pandu as well. How helpless was Kunti!

She must retain her strength, must get empowered... must be a procreator. She could not leave Pandu or ignore him or go against him. Pandu would give her sons and so would give her rights too.

50

"Bhishma!" Satyavati looked awfully frustrated. "Your guess was wrong. Pandu persists in his decision to march. Madri's charm has failed to stop him."

Bhishma was deeply concerned. He turned to Ambalika to ask whether Pandu had shared any details with her.

"No!" was Ambalika's depressed response.

"Pandu seems to have taken after you," Satyavati confronted Bhishma. "You also are not moved by a woman's charm. So is Pandu. He is leaving two beautiful young wives behind to pursue his universal conquest."

Here was a clue for Bhishma. He discerned an inkling of truth in Satyavati's observation. Was sensual pleasure a virtual torture to Pandu? Was feminine charm a mirage to him too? But he did attend Kunti's swayamvara and agreed to marry her! Why? He does get attracted to the feminine beauty but is instantly repulsed when he comes close to her. Was it due to his pride?

Bhishma was never convinced of Satyavati's logic. Her system of logic did not conform to any rule but was governed by self-interest. She only spoke and never heard others. And, most significantly, the rights she herself had gained as a woman and as a wife, she was not willing to concede to her daughters-in-law or grand-daughters-in-law. When empowered or capacitated, a woman's exploitation of another woman got more accelerated and intensified.

"With due permission, sir, I would like to submit a point too." It was now Ambalika, quite mild and subdued. "If Pandu is prompted by his pride to march on the universal conquest, I will wish him a victor's return and a happy life with his queens looking after his subjects. But, sire, if there is a discord between him and his wives, please don't arrange more wives for him."

"Don't you want a prince for Hastinapur?" Satyavati intervened.

"Gandhari can give you a prince, mother! No throne in the world has ever remained unoccupied. Every throne would select the heir. While the crown princes are waiting, the throne itself moves ahead and picks up its own occupant."

Bhishma eyed Ambalika: the suffering personified!

"Won't you like your grandson occupying the throne of Hastinapur?" he said.

"I will be pleased. I am also a pack of human desires. But the world has suffered a lot by burning with desire. Sometimes, someone burns in desire and sometimes someone's desire burns others. I have much suffered that burn. I no more want anyone else to endure the burn of my desires and curse this world. Don't you feel the Kuru dynasty is already overburdened with deserted women? Have mercy on me and don't add to that burden by any means."

She choked and hurried away.

Gandhari was gladsomely gay. "Noble One!" she said, "You know, devar is marching on a universal conquest."

"Yes, I have so heard," Dhritrashtra replied. "But why should you be so interested, dear?"

"Why shouldn't I?" Gandhari laughed. "He will conquer kingdoms, expand the Kuru empire, and fetch a lot of wealth and slave girls."

"And deposit it all with you?"

"No, bestow it all upon Kunti and Madri whom he has not returned to after the one first night."

"Why should Pandu behave like that? What else does he want? Both the girls are pretty. Even otherwise, no one restrains him if he desires to get some other. I am happy that way. Beautiful or ugly, that makes no difference to me. I cannot see. I know by touch that it is a woman. And that is enough for me."

"Be quiet and now listen to what I say."

"Something special?

"You may not think so. But I don't believe his quest for a universal conquest is genuine. After Kunti, if even Madri has failed to attract and bind him beyond the first night, there must be something wrong with him. He cannot face his wife."

"You mean Pandu is impotent."

"Exactly."

"Which means Pandu will marry again."

"Devar may marry once or a hundred times more; he will not beget an heir. Hastinapur will not have a crown prince from him."

"How can you be so sure?"

"Shakuni has told me."

Dhritrashtra did not feel sorry for his impotent brother. He was rather glad with Gandhari. He might be sightless but he was not impotent like Pandu who, though a king, was not a complete man. If Gandhari was right about Pandu, Dhritrashtra was far better and more capable than him. Dhritrashtra would produce so many children that the Kuru dynasty would be known only by his name in future.

"You will see, Noble One," Gandhari reiterated. "Our son will inherit the crown of Hastinapur after Pandu."

Dhritrashtra rejoiced in that proclamation.

51

Kunti was astonished at Madri's visit. She resented her presence, her very existence. In fact, she never wished to see Madri. She held Madri guilty of consenting to marry Pandu even as she was aware of his first wife and that he had abandoned her the very first-nuptial night.

Kunti indicted Madri more than she did Pandu. If a woman chose to be atrocious to another woman, the man was not responsible in any way.

Kunti's maiden encounter with her rival happened when she was ushered in by the maid. She was immediately struck by Madri's beauty! But why was she so dishevelled! Kunti wondered.

Though almost the same age, Kunti admitted she was senior to Madri for being Pandu's first wife.

What Kunti heard from Madri seemed to be a repeat of her own story. The same grand reception, the same expectations betrayed on the first night.

Kunti listened with rapt attention. She interrogated Madri: "Were you aware of my presence as Pandu's wife before you were married off?"

"Yes."

"Why did you then consent to marry him?"

"Consent!" Madri was puzzled. "But no one asked for my consent. I was simply given away to Pitravya Bhishma by my brother."

"And your brother, didn't he know that the king was

already married?"

"Maybe, he knew it. But that hardly matters when polygamy is in vogue across the land... Moreover, Pitravya Bhishma had the four-winged army with him. Anything could happen otherwise."

So we are sailing in the same boat-Madri and I, Kunti said to herself.

They were both the victims of circumstances, both were helpless, both needed someone to support them. They should not engage in any rivalry but be each other's prop. If the deprived offended each other, no one would come forward to help them. A mutual regard might sometime win them their rights.

Madri said, "I am with you. I will do your bidding."

"We are not against but with each other," Kunti concluded. "Whatever we secure in life, we will have it together. We won't obtain anything at the cost of the other."

"I fully agree with you, Didi (elder sister)!" Madri was blissfully content as she embraced Kunti.

52

Bhishma found himself at the Kauravas' military camp.

He was there to persuade Pandu a last time to quit his idea of combat and spend at least a couple of years with his new-found consorts, produce a great grandson for Mother Satyavati and heir to the throne of Hastinapur and enthrone him, after which he could march on his proposed battle of universal conquest.

However, the ambience at the cantonment and a discourse with Pandu frustrated his noble intent. Pandu was adamant and all pleas fell flat on his ears.

It was the same pride that had been beguiling Pandu all through. Pandu stood there as if he was in the middle of a war.

"Our adversaries think the Kuru dynasty is left with no warrior now. They think you have grown old and cannot fight. Bhaiya (brother) Dhritrashtra is born blind and, they presume I am sick, imbecile and coward and what not. I want to show them the valour of the Kuru kings has not at all diminished. The forces of Hastinapur are as strong as ever."

"My son! This is not a sign of your gallantry but of barbarism," Bhishma quipped.

"How do you know?" Pandu was taken aback. "I could not reveal it thus far. I was not sure who to tell. But I am overwhelmed with thoughts of violence. Sire! I am becoming a savage beast now. I feel I will tear apart anyone who happens to confront me. Hence this march for universal conquest. I will pick up an enemy, challenge him and bestow all my bestiality upon him. I fear that if I do any such act here then how would I go about explaining it to all and sundry."

Bhishma saw the futility of any further arguments.

However, as a last resort, he said, "you have two brides at home. Don't they inspire any love in you?"

"No, sire," Pandu replied. "They provoke me to be violent. I feel, if I stayed any longer with them, I will lose my equilibrium and commit some obnoxious offence."

53

"Kunti! How are you, bahu (daughter-in-law)?" Ambalika said, "How do you feel about all these news about your husband's military exploits-his combats and conquests?"

What to say! Kunti had never had that wifely feeling for the man Ambalika referred to. His conquests had no meaning to her. She never thought she had a husband who was currently away from her... that he was engaged in battle... winning... And he could even be vanquished. It was all insignificant to her.

She cherished an altogether different set of questions which she asked herself or her Creator. .

What prompted her to choose Pandu as her husband? Thus, she had imprisoned herself in all willingness and consciousness into that citadel of Hastinapur.

Once, pricked by a singular complex of not being a king himself, his father Shursena had offered her to King Kuntibhoja. Was history being replicated in Kunti's life? Her father had anticipated that she would be reared as a princess. And she prompted the reversal of the wheel of time by selecting Pandu, the king, at first sight. She, an adopted daughter of an ordinary king, was anon swept off her feet in his imposing presence.

"Pandu has vanquished several kings. He has caused some damage to the Panchalas, killed a king of South Magadha and conquered the Videhas. Aren't you impressed, pleased?" Ambalika asked Kunti.

Kunti had no genuine answer to that. She was rather scared that she might be exposed.

"Don't fear me, my daughter!" Ambalika was all affection. "I am Pandu's mother but you may regard me as your mother and not as your mother-in-law. I was here to beg your pardon."

Pardon! Wherefore?

"For my son's misconduct, my daughter!" Ambalika opened up. "I am here to know whether you have quarreled or it was only history repeating itself ... And did he come close to you?"

"Nothing of that sort.He tried to be close, but distanced himself at the crucial moment," Kunti disclosed.

So Ambalika's doubts were not misplaced. "He will be returning with a lot of wealth," she said, "But you two, his queens-you and Madri-you two will continue to be penurious. It is the common fate of the queens of the Kurus. In Hastinapur, history would repeat itself like that... And I am here also to reassure you... If you ever find your afflictions unendurable, you may frankly come to me... I am immensely capable of that."

And Ambalika left.

Kunti, though puzzled at Ambalika's real purpose of visit, was at least enlightened that her mother-in-law, a queen mother, was not happy.

But Kunti was made of a different stuff. She was the daughter of the Yadavas! She was brought up under the stringent discipline of King Kuntibhoja. She was prepared for any plight and adversities. Her brother Vasudeva and bhabhi (sister-in-law) Devaki were still in Kansa's custody and no one dared confront Kansa on that point. And her brother's kids were being put to death in succession.

To Kunti, a child could compensate for her husband's indifference. If Pandu had behaved so after giving her a child, she would never complain.

And that reminded her of a new-born baby boy. Her

father, Kuntibhoja, had given him off to a nurse. He was here in Hastinapur... at the household of Adhiratha, a charioteer. But his whereabouts were obscure. Could she locate him without raising doubts?

Who knew what lay in store for Kunti!

54

Pandu was back in Hastinapur to a grand warm reception. He had returned with a huge booty from the conquered kings and a large pack of captured soldiers. He had paid formal visits to Bhishma, Satyavati, his mother, and gifted them immensely.

Kunti heard about that from others for he did not summon her nor did she go to see him. She had sunk into impassivity and nothing affected her. She felt she could endure anything. She had stayed at a loving but stringent disciplinarian's palace as his daughter, away from her real parents. She had appeased the irritable sage Durvasa in spite of herself. She had abandoned her new-born son in order to maintain the honour of her father. And, now she had no grudge having to spend the rest of her days as the abandoned, disgraced wife of Pandu. Maybe God had created her for such experiments. He had moulded her as a crag to withstand the gushes of violent streams.

It was amidst such thoughts that Kunti was informed, "Maharani! The king is coming."

What? Really? Finally, he could spare time for her? Did he really care for her, love her?

Let Pandu be here. Kunti would receive him with open arms. She was very generous. She had the forbearance to forgive and forget all, and start afresh in her relations.

Finally, Pandu stepped into Kunti's chamber.

"Did you ever miss me there?" Kunti said.

"There is no time for such thoughts on the battlefield," Pandu was impassioned." It was not a petty combat. It was quite a series of battles! It was what they call a universal conquest. A digvijay in the real sense. The soldiers fight, get tired, injured or sick, but a king can do nothing but fight, tirelessly fight... I have demonstrated to all those kings what a kshatriya is and what we really mean by a battle... You may see why bhaiya Dhritrashtra was not made the king! ... A king he could of course be, but not a warrior, which is primary requirement for a king. How could he, born-blind as he is, take the field and wield arms?"

His bragging seemed ceaseless. Food was brought and lovingly served by Kunti but Pandu was not interested in eating. He would talk his heart out.

"The Panchalas will never dare stare us in our face. I have given a fitting reply to Drupada. I have driven down their entire livestock."

Kunti waited for him to finish. She sat close to Pandu on the bed.

Pandu observed her. "You look a shade or two pale," he said. "Have you been worrying too much in my absence?"

"Obviously! Shouldn't I be worrying when you are out on the field?"

"If warriors' wives worry, how would the husbands fight without worries?"

"You mean a warrior's wife shouldn't even care to love him?" Kunti flirted.

"A hero's life is very crucial," Pandu was excited. "On the one side the enemies strike with swords and on the other there are beauties with their murderous looks."

"You should have come here with your armour on to protect yourself from the beauties' arrows."

"If I did that my heart would curse the armour for not allowing the arrows to pierce it..."

And he gathered her in an embrace so passionate and

tight that she gasped, "You stifle me, my hero! Are you courting your sweetheart or smashing the bones of an enemy?"

Pandu's response was horrifying. His eyes bulged out and he looked more tortured than stimulated. His embrace slackened. He panted and he struggled to ward off the excruciating pain he was evidently suffering.

It was the same as on that first night! Kunti was baffled. Was it common with him on such moments of intimacy, Kunti wondered. Was this why he left his two pretty brides and strove to act gallant in far-off lands! He wanted to eclipse his defeat in the bed by a 'victory on the field'!

Slightly recomposed, he gathered himself up and prepared to leave.

"Why! Where do you go?"

"It is about Vidur's wedding. I have an urgent piece of work."

Kunti looked on as Pandu walked out.

55

"Paransavi!" Vidur was humble and soft in his speech. "Hope you are aware of my position in the Kuru family!"

So very unanticipated! Paransavi had, though, heard about her husband. He was very learned, grave, religious, righteous and gentle. The people had very high opinion of him.

Still, it was their first night. Whatever his intellectual status or acumen, a husband was essentially a man who must talk about love and charm.

Instead her husband queried about his position in the Kuru family. What did he expect from her? What would she say?

"You are the king's brother," she eventually spoke up.

"Yes. But when it came to the kingship of Hastinapur, Dhritrashtra was the first consideration being the eldest; however, his blindness by birth disqualified him. As for Pandu, though thoroughly noble, he is sick with a nervous tension that makes him most unstable and unpredictable. As such, he also should have been kept out of consideration. But since I am born of a maid, I was not conceded equal rights. We three brothers were married by the honourable uncle Bhishma but he acted scrupulously. While he chose princesses for Dhritrashtra and Pandu, for me he got a king's daughter but from a maid. Mind it, I am, of course, King Pandu's brother, but I am not fathered by Vichitravirya!"

"You regret that?" Paransavi was frank. "You resent your wife being a maid's daughter and not a princess?"

"Never!" Vidur smiled. He put his caring hands on her shoulders. "I was just trying to explain my and your position in the Kuru family, in life, and in society, so that you don't harbour very high expectations. I am blessed to have you for my wife. I inherit some of my progenitor Vyasadeva's attributes. I least aspire to be a kshatriya. I abhor war. I am all for peace. Peace for all the creatures in this world. I have preferably worked to detect the causes of war, the form and the consequences of war. Can war make man happy? Don't you want to be happy, Paransavi?"

"Who wouldn't, my Noble One?"

"Then, listen, my lady! Happy can be one who encounters reality and accepts it, for happiness lies not in physical situations, but in mental conditioning. I have accepted my peculiar position in this family. That I am both a part of it and not a part of it. Though I am a brother to Dhritrashtra and Pandu, the family wealth is not mine. And I don't desire it. Acquiring another person's wealth would not make anyone happy or fetch him peace of mind. A sage renounces everything and is still happy whereas a king possesses everything and is still unhappy. Hence I say: give one what is his. It would make both happy-the receiver and the giver. All the quarrels, differences and wars will be eliminated from this world if all are given what is lawfully theirs."

How erudite! Paransavi was proud of her husband. A new panorama of information unfolded for her.

About Dhritrashtra, strange facts were revealed to her. She learnt he was after Hastinapur's kingdom. He aspired for the enjoyment of power! In spite of his sightlessness!

"Well! He is sightless but he has no restraint besides," Vidur said. "He's not aware what havoc the senses could play when unleashed... He instigates Pandu to stay out of Hastinapur on various pretexts so that Dhritrashtra could have his own way with the affairs of the kingdom. And his confidant... That cunning, lecherous Shakuni, he is sure to bring devastation to the Kuru clan."

"But Pandu! Can't he see through all that?" Paransavi quizzed.

"Of course, he does. But he has his own set of weaknesses which he is not able to get better of," Vidur replied.

Paransavi was scared for her husband. Wasn't he scared?

"The lower classes are scared for their livelihood, the middle classes of death and the superior ones are scared only of a bad name."

Then, becoming conscious of the delicacy of the occasion, he came closer to her, touched her amorously. He was apologetic about his lack of romanticism.

"A lover's love is swift and passionate, like a hilly river! And the husband's love is deep and profound like the waters of the Ganga. It may not sweep away but surely takes you across."

"I do understand," Paransavi said, "but, my noble one, even the Ganga is inundated."

"Yes," Vidur laughed. "And, I hope you will not fear the overwhelming flow of my love, my learned sweetheart!"

"A last point-I am also a maid's daughter. Your mother was a maid in her early days too. Will this fact bring dishonour upon us in society?" Paransavi said.

"A wicked one, howsoever high-born, is always denied respect and a righteous one is ultimately honoured," Vidur minced no words. "Respect comes not from wealth, learning, renown or from belonging to a certain clan; respect comes but from conduct, my lady! Thus, I value probity the most. And my clan was not chosen by me. It was allotted by the social system. Why should I then be ashamed? Nor should you be apologetic about your birth. We are far, far better than the many high-born kshatriya aristocrats around us."

56

Kunti's maids rushed about for a couple of days, looking out for Pandu.

As long as the celebrations of Vidur's weddings were on, tracing him was not easy.

When the occasional din subsided, the maids appeared with the news that the king was about to leave for forest a-hunting. Hectic preparations were on in the chariot stand and the stable. The king seemed to be in an inexplicable hurry to be out of Hastinapur.

Kunti was at once fuming and frustrated. She groped for some rationale behind his demeanour. And what was her fault?

The next moment, she straightened up. She would gain nothing by crying. No one was going to share her plight. Pandu would chariot away to forest and kill the innocent beings while she would be left behind to fret and fume in frustration. Was it in that manner she would be living out her life?

No way! She also came from a kshatriya stock. She also had the right to live. Life did not offer anything on a platter and gave nothing even on asking. You had to strive for that.

She was stalled in her track of thoughts by Madri's visit.

Madri was looking for Pandu and was sorely distressed. Kunti did whatever she could to calm her.

"Madri!" she said, "you know, in the society we are reared in, man can thus humiliate a woman. He can neglect us to have relations with others and marry another woman. But once we have accepted a man as our husband, we are left with no choice. We may be loved by him, spurned or deserted by him, be his widow or die with him as sati, but we will be his ... we must learn to accept our situation."

She proposed that either they should approach Pandu or Ambalika or Bhishma for a redressal.

"Why them?" Madri dissented. "If I must, I will beg my husband."

The two queens found Pandu at the stable,selecting horses for hunting.

It was settled that the stable was not a proper place to discuss their private matters.

Pandu drove them to his portion of the palace and commanded privacy.

He was visibly nervous. He had never encountered the two queens at once before.

He tried to explain that the Aryan kings tended to go on hunting excursions. They bravely face the enemy in combat and the fierce animals in hunting.

"Do they ever face their wife or always show their back to her?" Madri's burst was sudden and sharp. "Don't ever deceive us with your kshatriya descent and gallantry. Talk about your manly prowess. How long will you escape from Hastinapur?"

Pandu was outraged.

Kunti offered to assuage him. "We don't mean to disgrace you," she said. "All we desire is let us three assess our problem and together find out a solution."

"What problem?" Pandu demanded.

"The only problem is, Noble One," Kunti said, "that you are away from us on this pretext or that, engaging in the pursuit of a universal conquest or hunting. How shall we be gratified? Agreed, we can't be with you on a combat, but at least we can accompany you to the game?"

"Game! Women are not required there. You can't wield a weapon, nor have you any courage to confront the fierce beasts. Will you hunt me there?"

"That's our resolve!" Kunti smiled.

"No! That'll be inconvenient," Pandu resisted. "Will I go a-hunting or protect you? I don't engage in such miraculous acts."

"But you perform the wonder of running away from the beds of beautiful dames in distress," rejoined Madri.

"Wait, Madri," Kunti intercepted and, turning to Pandu, submitted, "O brave, Noble One! If you and your brave soldiers can't protect two young women from some beasts, your game is a sham. Better you don a brahmin's attire. We have resolved to be with you in the forest. Why, Madri?"

"Yes," Madri seconded her. "And if you refuse, we will approach the venerable Bhishma."

Pandu was disarmed. "Well, you may come along," he said. "But, mind you, I am going there to hunt, not to entertain you. So you shall not disturb me in that."

"Your instruction will be honoured," Kunti endorsed softly.

57

Bhishma observed Dhritrashtra's eagerness to send off Pandu on hunting. Dhritrashtra not only oversaw the relevant arrangements but even dispatched several of his own attendants with him who, Bhishma knew, were Dhritrashtra's confidants whose job was to gather and send back secret information about Pandu. In fact, Dhritrashtra intended to provide Pandu with such a mass of comforts so that the latter would never miss his palace.

What was Dhritrashtra's intention? Was he spinning some political conspiracy against Pandu? Did he want Pandu mostly out of Hastinapur? Wasn't he acquiring more and more autonomy aided by Gandhari and Shakuni?

Why was the one who was invalid chasing power and the genuinely deserving one did not find it so essential? Bhishma could apprehend Dhritrashtra's case but why was Pandu so frequently away from Hastinapur? He had been avoiding and ignoring his first wife Kunti and then also the second one, Madri. But now he had taken both of them to excursion! Why! was he treading in the foot-steps of King Shantanu who was wont to wandering disoriented in forests and on riversides? But Shantanu was forlorn for his wife had left him. And Pandu? Bhishma was puzzled. He discerned the handiwork of Kama (the deity of sensual desire) behind that.

Satyavati summoned Bhishma to discuss it with him. She was most anxious about Pandu.

"Why?"

"Primarily because after your father, he is the first full-fledged king who occupies the throne of Hastinapur with complete authority, who is fully grown-up, mature, independent, and capable of wielding power."

"But that must please you!"

"Definitely. But he would not stick to Hastinapur most of the time."

"Still a king is best seen touring his kingdom, seeing places, meeting his subjects."

"But he indulges in conflicts and hunting, both of which are threatening. Seems to be resenting himself. Like Chitrangada,he is often daring others... I hear he has so harassed the Panchalas that they have turned the bitterest enemies of the Kurus."

Bhishma dismissed Satyavati's apprehensions. He even defended Pandu when she said, "And now he is on to hunting, to defy lions and other fierce beasts. He has taken his two brides along! Seems he has gone mad."

"Not gone mad, mother. He has just got married. A kshatriya enjoys life in entirety. He takes the whole and gives up the whole. Let them enjoy life," Bhishma said.

"Which could have been enjoyed here as well," Satyavati sounded anxious. "Here they have palaces, attendants, dames, foods and wine. What else would they need?"

"Here they have all grades of relations, kingly liabilities and crowd," Bhishma laughed. "Here they cannot have unhurdled living or behaving. There they will be free as Nature's beings."

"And they leave behind this rascal Dhritrashtra and that seasoned sinner Shakuni here in Hastinapur," Satyavati fumed.

"Why should you oppose them, mother?"

"Aren't you aware that in Dhritrashtra's hands no maid is safe and around Shakuni no one except gamblers and drunkards could possibly exist. If these vices join hands, what ill would be spared, son? There will be murders and rapes. When rulers are such debauchers, where would one seek justice? Can Dhritrashtra quote a day when he has not lied or made a false promise? Making false promises and giving false assurances has been assumed the ruler's birth-right."

"Therefore do I say," Satyavati resumed. "Recall Pandu immediately. Even if he won't prosecute these rascals, he would at least not indulge in such villainous acts himself."

"I will try, mother!" Bhishma said.

58

The workmen had pitched the camp ahead of their king's and two queens' arrival and everything looked spick and span.

Kunti and Madri took their places in the pavilion reserved for them and Pandu said, "relax yourselves here. I'll go and see other arrangements."

Madri tried to be sportive but was silenced by Pandu's cutting remark and Kunti's gesture.

As Pandu darted out, Madri spewed her irritation.

"Madri!" Kunti offered to appease her. "I appreciate your anguish. I am enduring the same. Please have patience and try to understand him. I feel he is fighting not us but his own self ... More so, we have to get used to him as with him we have to spend our life. Let us do it with utmost grace and normalcy. Try to like this camp, this temporary residence!"

Kunti and her pleas only puzzled Madri.

Pandu returned at the dusk.

His appearance incensed Madri: "Is it recreation or imprisonment! You dump us here and vanish into the blue!" she said.

Pandu was irritated: "We are here for hunting and not for any excursion. This terrain is starkly difficult and I must make your stay comfortable here."

"We were not short of comfort back in Hastinapur. Why are we here?"

Madri's outburst was managed by Kunti who requested Pandu not to bother about them. "We are here to avail of your company and, denied that, we will not enjoy any hunting," she submitted to him.

"In that case, you may return to Hastinapur. I was here to inform you that I am leaving again and you don't have to wait for me at meal nor will you try to call for me."

True to his words, Pandu did not appear for meal.

Madri felt all the more insulted. She threatened to kill herself.

"Which anyone can do any time," Kunti smiled.

"Don't take it lightly!" Madri said. "I either live on my own terms or I die."

"I'm not taking you any lightly, Madri," Kunti said. "I think it is better to turn life in one's own favour than to terminate it. Conditioning life in your favour requires a lot of endurance and courage."

"You think I am not enduring?" Madri protested.

"A little altercation or difference with your husband-that is no suffering, no endurance! I don't intend to belittle your distress. Still... I am a Yadava woman. The Yadavas have been and still are subjected to a great lot of torture and atrocity. My brother and sister-in-law are imprisoned by Kansa who is killing their newborn babies. Is your humiliation at your husband's hands any greater? This life is immense and multi-faceted. Everything in it is not necessarily favourable to a person. Pride and prestige are not eternal. What is eternal is effort, incessant industry, invincible faith, steadfast intellect and conscience."

Madri was genuinely moved by Kunti's tale of woes: Her rearing at King Kuntibhoja's palace away from her real parents, about her brother and sister-in-law; about her husband's treatment which Madri had also been a party to.

Pandu was back around the mid-night hour.

"You must be tired. So am I. It is again hunting early in the morning. Sleep now." These words were addressed to Madri and Kunti who, though awake, chose not to respond.

Sleep eluded Pandu too. He had deliberately exhausted himself so that he would fall asleep the moment he lay down in bed. He wished to be oblivious to his surroundings, his relation with them, and their expectations from him.

His state of such occasional insomnia pushed him into a sort of insanity.

He lay assessing his own self in contrast with Dhritrashtra and Vidur, the former was over-interested in bedding young girls despite being sightless and the other overly intellectual.

As for himself, Pandu knew he was to be a king, for which he had to be a warrior first, and training in arms had never been difficult for him. He was surrounded by countless maids and other dames who were his for asking.

But then he learnt about his impotence.

After his marriage with Kunti, his inability to consummate had tortured him to extreme. He had consulted the royal physician, who declared:

"Your Majesty! Your weak nerves may not endure the excitement. You are advised to stay away from the real act and take regular medicine. Some rest and medicine may rejuvenate you enough to indulge in occasional congress. In your present condition, the act may prove fatal for you."

Therefore Pandu had planned the digvijay, the universal conquest, thinking that would allow him to keep off Kunti and also take medicine regularly. But, Sire Bhishma's misjudgement pushed him into a mirage called Madri.

However, his universal conquest had changed nothing on that crucial front. He had returned without any improvement in his condition. His nerves failed him yet again. He could satisfy neither Kunti nor Madri. He had to leave the two in utter humiliation.

Yet his pride would not admit defeat. He was a man, young and brave, the king of Hastinapur! How could he confess to his wives, to his subjects, to his family and mentors that he was without that vital virility?

His impotent rage kept him wide awake and he left quite early, without any escorts or armed support. He would kill or get killed! He ventured into the dense forest.

A few paces from him he detected a pair of deer engaged in coition. Pandu could not stand it. How could this pair of petty beings perform what he, a superior man, could not! He would not allow any being in this world the pleasure he himself was not capable of deriving.

He pulled out an arrow from his quiver, let it fly in that direction, and the next moment the deer lay writhing beside his partner. The doe was distraught and, as the gravity of situation sunk in, jumped into the overgrowth and disappeared.

He approached the deer who lay lifeless, his mouth distorted by the signature of act. This was Pandu's act of violence that had finished it for the deer and separated the doe who were enjoying the most enviable pleasure of life not long ago. But, what was Pandu's gain? What was Pandu's aim? To have pleasure, or to deprive other beings of that pleasure? Violence had never made one happy.

Pandu could no longer stay beside the deer. No living deer had ever taught him the mysteries of life as this dead one was doing.

Pandu lost track of his camp. He forgot about Kunti and Madri, the soldiers and the attendants, the male and maid servants. He roamed about disoriented and demented.

Soonhe found himself near a hermitage where he saw a group of forest-dwelling ascetics, cottages and heard the chanting of sweet mantras. This was Kindama rishi's ashram. The smoke from the sacrificial fire was inviting.

Pandu's weapons fell from his hands, he dragged himself to where the inmates were assembled and sat down behind them.

Prayers over, the Kulpati looked up and said, "Hail you King Pandu! I, Kindama, welcome you to my ashram."

"You recognised me, Kulpati!" Pandu exclaimed as he stood up, his hands clasped in veneration.

"I was told you are here for game but never knew you would be here so early for worship. Hope you are happy."

Pandu fell upon the sage's feet, tears rolled down his eyes, "Where is the happiness?"

"Why, in the game!"

"I was not here for game. I just came here to forget my woes. I was running away from myself. Hunting was just an excuse."

"Come to my cottage."

Pandu followed him into his hut.

"Must be one of this ashram's deer," The rishi said upon Pandu's confession. "It did not escape for these deer are accustomed to human presence. You have committed a grave offence. These are not game."

"I admit my mistake. I am ready to atone. How do I get rid of this suffering?"

"Just as that deer got suffering, let in through desire, ends in death."

"Which means happiness is a non-entity?" Pandu said.

"What we call happiness is but a rapid degeneration of the life-force. That deer was your teacher and guide, who paid with his life to teach you a secret of life-that letting go of desire is the only way to peace. Desiring happiness is the cause of death. Happiness and suffering are the two aspects of truth. To attain peace, you have to give up happiness along with suffering. Desire is suffering; lust is torture; sensual desire is death-avoid it and you get a glorious life like Bhishma. As for the deer, it is now yours to use it any way you like."

Pandu did not retrieve the deer, nor his arms. He went back straight to his camp. He was resolved to share his new-found truth with others and to propagate it.

"I am relinquishing this householder's life; I will be a renouncer," he declared to Kunti and Madri.

"What about your wives?" Kunti asked.

"A renouncer has no wives, no relations. My father had abandoned me. I have abandoned my mother and brothers. I have no children. As for my wives, I sever my union with them. I will live a life of reclusion. I will do penance. The bodily pleasure I was denied; I will now seek the spiritual bliss."

"Where do you propose to accomplish it?"

"I will dwell in mountains, in forests anywhere. Wherever I relish to be."

"Where shall we go? Myself and Madri?"

"Go back to your parents."

"No married Aryan woman has done that," Kunti protested. "Never without her husband. Even Sita did not return to her parents for childbirth."

"Go to Hastinapur then."

"I will dwell with you."

"You don't approve of my decision to renounce?"

"But why do you seek to renounce? The sages recommend it at the age of seventy-five years. You are too young for that. Even Pitravya Bhishma has not gone into it."

"My father Vedvyasa is a recluse since his very childhood."

"He is a sage's child, not a king's." Kunti contended. "And, why should you renounce? Do you find any defect in our conduct, any lack in our person? Do we deprive you in any way?"

"No, Kunti. I don't find any fault in either of you.

The fault actually lies in me. I cannot be a father. I am not a complete husband. I am not capable of the conjugal bliss. I cannot endure it any longer. Renunciation is the only way out for me."

"Were you not aware of that before marriage?"

"No, I never imagined it."

"I understand you plight and pain. But I don't agree with you. If one of the spouses is ill, shall the other one concede separation? No, that will not do. Husbands get multilated in war. Do the women relinquish them? No, they are rather proud of their man. Carnal pleasure is not my wont. I simply crave your company. Nothing else. Which is more virtuous and honourable than leaning upon a kin's compassion and grace. And you are not what you think yourself to be. You need to apply diligence."

"What do you mean?" Pandu said.

"You should aspire to undertake penance, and not reclusion, which would imply separation-from your family,

society, your kingdom, and your rights. Then, Dhritrashtra will be the king of Hastinapur and you will never be entitled to a reclamation. In that case, even your son, if you miraculously beget one, will not inherit the kingdom. On the other hand, if Dhritrashtra fathers a son he will get the throne and not your son. So, don't contemplate reclusion. Don't forgo your rights."

Pandu was impressed. Kunti was wisely right. Rama spent fourteen years in exile but he retained his right to rule and was coronated on his return to Ayodhya.

Pandu saw wisdom in Kunti's advice. He must exercise diligence, do penance. Maybe, through the sages' company, by some great soul's grace, with treatment from the physicians at some ashram, he acquired such energy in his body and spirit that would cure his impotence, he would become a husband, a father. Could he then retreat to a householder's life? Never. Once a recluse, always a recluse.

Pandu paced about and pondered over the recent

developments.

"Madri! Do you agree with her?" He turned to Madri, who looked amazed. And, then to Kunti, decisively, "I step out to inform them of my decision to embrace penance. I will order them to march back to Hastinapur and register that we three are retiring to the Himalayas. Hastinapur shall wait until the penance is over."

And he went out.

Madri scoffed at Kunti for her 'lopsided' decision.

"I don't consider this marriage valid," Madri said. "I don't wish to embrace the life of penance. I will not live with an impotent husband. This is not justified. Why should a woman accept it the way the man liked? Is a woman not a human being? Is she an object? A lifeless rock?"

"I agree with you," Kunti pleaded. "But, be considerate. You were virtually purchased to be Pandu's wife. You have nowhere to go, no person to go to now!"

"Then, a woman has no right?"

"A mother has, a woman doesn't. You have the examples of grandma Satyavati and Amba before you. That's why I talk of social justice. You have to accept it. There is no option for now," Kunti declared.

59

Ambalika received Ambika cordially in her chamber. It was a long deferred visit.

"Why should Pandu do this?" Ambika started, "Renunciation at this age!"

"He has not renounced," Ambalika said. "He has gone to do penance, just as earlier he had gone for a universal conquest and then for game. He will be back once the penance is over."

"Still it was plainly uncalled for at this age. The grandmother enjoys life in palaces, the old pitravya oversees governance and the grandson is off to penance in a forest. Isn't it abnormal?" Ambika muttered.

"It is the norm in this family," Ambalika contended. "The aged ones survive and the kids meet an untimely death. The juniors issue commands from the seat and the seniors obey them. Everything is topsy-turvy here. Strange that in Hastinapur, the Ganga does not flow from the ocean to the Himalayas!"

Ambika said, "Dhritrashtra says Pandu has renounced, which means Pandu will never return to Hastinapur and since he has no son, Dhritrashtra will occupy the throne so long as a son of Dhritrashtra comes of age to look after the kingdom... I doubt whether Dhritrashtra has urged Pandu on to penance. He has been doing such pranks since a very young age to keep Pandu off the exploits of governance."

"It hardly matters, Didi," Ambalika was not affected.

"It does matter, Ambalika," asserted Ambika. "Since my childhood, I have been turning a blind eye to circumstances. And it went on until Vedvyasa's appearance as the appointed man."

"Then?"

"Then I stopped that practice and woke up to recognise diligence and effort. When he came the next time, I sent Maryada over to him. I have stopped shutting my eyes since then. Therefore have I come here to warn you that you shall never assume that Pandu has gone over to penance for good. I will never have Dhritrashtra believe he is the sole king of Hastinapur whose right there is none to dispute... Otherwise, he will go unbridled. Pandu shouldn't have gone. He and Vidur together would have restrained Dhritrashtra... Now I am looking up to Vidur. I don't suggest my Dhritrashtra is innocent. My point of concern is that this Shakuni is actuating his vices. Shakuni is popularising gambling in Hastinapur. He is getting it patronised through Dhritrashtra, making it a prestigious form of recreation. The result? In the state assembly, the gamblers will command more respect than the learned ones."

"You refer to Hastinapur," Ambalika said. "I hear drinking and gambling are becoming more and more honourable in all the royal families. Why be concerned about Dhritrashtra then?"

"For he is under the obnoxious influence of the gambler-king Shakuni," Ambika replied. "Adultery, drinking, wickedness, cheating-every vice is making inroads into Hastinapur through gambling ... And we can do nothing about it, for Queen Gandhari's brother Shakuni is loving it. This brother-in-law of the king is the very epitome of what can be evil."

"What is this the maids are talking about!" Gandhari complained, "That you have today ordered in the council that emissaries from Hastinapur should keep approaching Pandu wherever he is and exchange information with him and supply essentials for him, Kunti and Madri."

"What's wrong in that?" Dhritrashtra countered. "The master of politics Kanik exhorts us to remain informed of even our enemies, whereas Pandu is my brother."

Gandhari kept mum on that point for she had by now acquired the ability to read Dhritrashtra's mind.

After a studied silence, she said, "As the elder brother, you must ensure that your anchorite brother is not forced to ever return home. It is our duty to help him uphold his pledge."

"You are my ideal spouse," Dhritrashtra stretched out in bed. "If you really want to help me, give me at the earliest a son who I shall declare the crown prince of Hastinapur."

Gandhari walked up to Dhritrashtra and said, "I wish it too, O Noble One!"

Vidur returned home all exhausted and lay down. Paransavi was concerned.

"To be present at the council becomes increasingly tedious each coming day," Vidur explained. "The dirty discourses of Dhritrashtra, his brother-in-law Shakuni and their ministers stifle me. I would rather shun it all and go away."

"King Pandu has retreated to forest. Uncle Bhishma has lost interest," Paransavi said. "Now you talk of retiring from the council. Will that put a check upon these libertines in power? You have forsaken arms; at least, you should not forsake ethics."

"You are prudent in your advice," Vidur said. "I will stick to ethics. That will be my duty as a Kshatriya hence."

60

They had been walking since dawn, halting briefly when tired. Pandu had noticed that Kunti never grumbled about her tiredness whereas Madri had been unabashedly vocal, often asking, "When do we rest?" or "Should we not rest a while now?" Indeed, Madri was more delicate than Kunti but Kunti was the more resolute. Madri's gestures betrayed her fear that she was with them only because otherwise she would lose Pandu totally to Kunti.

Earlier they had dwelt at Mount Nagshsat where there was a hermit's ashram and several hamlets around so closely located that very often the mendicant inmates migrated to the clusters for a short sojourn. From there they had advanced through Mount Chaitraratha, Kalakoot, the Himalayas and Gandhanadana to the pond Indradyumna which fascinated Pandu and where they stayed for quite a few days. Their last resort was Mount Hansakoot, and now they were heading for Mount Shatashring.

Pandu felt fairly healthful and tranquil these days. Probably it was owing to the climate or the picturesque surroundings-these lofty hills; the exotic vegetation; the waving acres of flora; the exhilarating wind; the sporadic springs gushing out of the earth with melodious sounds. How so very contrasting from the narrowness of the palace at Hastinapur! The people there behaved like a multitude of children of the generous Mother Nature.

Their journey was gladly punctuated by these people's

uncreative invites and their consequent stay.

Pandu's conflict was dissolved and he felt light at heart. His relations with Kunti and Madri were normalised. Their proximity stirred no complexes in him. His violent thoughts were left far behind. He was now an all-new himself.

At dusk, they decided to reach the Shatashring ashram before the nightfall.

At the ashram, they were introduced to the master.

Pandu offered to observe strict celibacy. He said, "I will wear the tree bark, eat fruits and roots, and do penance in the forest. I will bathe twice, burn sacrificial fire, eat little, and emaciate myself. I will give up violence and live in solitude."

"Why should you need to be here to do penance? You could have done that at Hastinapur," the sage demanded.

"Hastinapur! There I was a king and kings are not celibates, master," Pandu submitted.

"So you have opted for celibacy against kingdom, which means you are no more a king? But why?"

Here was the question Pandu had been evading and because of which he had travelled so far from his people. He had admitted his impotence to Kunti and Madri but could he do that publicly?

"To get a child-the crown prince of Hastinapur," Pandu replied.

The sage smiled, "You have forsaken the kingdom but carry your love for it and perhaps the kingly pride too."

An elaborate discourse with the sage was enough to confound Pandu. He looked puzzled.

"This is sham, my son!" the master concluded. "Two young wives at your side, in your youth, you seek to observe celibacy! Go and ponder over what I have just said. When you arrive at a decision, tell me. You could possibly see me in the evening tomorrow."

A young celibate escorted them to their cottages, a separate hut for each of them.

Sleep eluded Madri for quite long. She had been brought up in a regal way and ambience. For this life of reclusion with an impotent husband! Her attention was drawn to Kunti who was also enduring the same. It was not Madri's independent decision; she had followed Kunti but had not yet accepted her decision or that system. What would Madri do with such a life! To her, enjoyment was life. The life ended for her the moment she was denied the enjoyment. The end of life she could comprehend but a halt of life she would not accept. But Kunti might be right in her assertion that where one is denied emotional justice, one must accept the social justice.

61

Pandu spent that sleepless night in contemplation: What did he want from his life?

Kunti had got up and bathed very early in the morning and after the combined prayer and sacrifice (yajna) she was busy with the female inmates making arrangements for children's meal. She looked very much a part of the ashram. No remnant of her being King Kuntibhoja's daughter could be traced.

As Pandu observed, life at the ashram was a community life, there was no 'individual' there. There were celibates and householders, both male and female. Nothing belonged exclusively to one individual. All belonged to the ashram as a community. Therefore, no one was solitary and helpless - all inclined to help one another.

At the ashram, commonality prevailed over the individual self. Nothing was personal. The duty was held supreme.

The total abnegation of self so common at the ashram was a far cry for Pandu. He could hardly forget he was the king of Hastinapur. His sporadic attempt at being ordinary triggered his pride and he concluded he would never succeed at that. But Kunti's spirit of servitude was spontaneous. She could easily shift from the mundane to the sublime. She was different.

At sundown, Pandu told the master, "I have been pondering over your discourse of yesterday. I must admit

I have renounced nothing-neither the kingship nor my craving for it. During the mission of the universal conquest and while on hunting, I was actually trying to evade my wives. I had not acknowledged my actuality then. However, my recent musings lead me to believe I am craving for a legitimate son!"

"You want a son, not sensual pleasure?"

"I want a legitimate son."

"Euphemism won't alter the facts."

"I will do all you ask me to beget a legitimate son."

"Seek refuge in nature. You may get blessed through a perpetual meditational practice. Observe abstinence. Consult able physicians. Nature might bestow upon you the strength present in every man. Then you will be able to enjoy it with your spouse and beget a legitimate son."

"How long will it take, O Great Sage?"

"Only God can tell. It may take a very long time and the end result may not necessarily be to your liking."

"In that case, I may not get my wish fulfilled and even lose my kingdom... To be frank, I have left my kingdom in care of my brother Dhritrashtra. If he begets a son before me, he will declare him the crown-prince. And beyond that, even my begetting a son will prove futile for my son will not get the kingdom then."

"If you want a son, you may resort to 'niyoga'. Let an accomplished man do it on your behalf."

62

His discourse with the master barely impressed Pandu. He was not happy. Initially, he cursed himself for his decision to migrate to this ashram from Hastinapur where he could enjoy all amenities as a king. A son through 'niyoga'! Another man procreating for him! Why, that could be managed in Hastinapur itself! He wished to return there and make amends.

Pandu, nevertheless, mulled over the sage's proposal. He thought about his father Vichitravirya. But he was not there to see that his wives were lying with another man. How would Pandu let it happen despite himself? Would his heart not break? Or would he not get outraged and hit that 'appointed' man?

To cool down, Pandu put his head under the cold stream and was detected by the Ayurvedacharya who chastised him for that indiscreet act. He checked Pandu's pulse and diagnosed, "Your nervous system is weak. Don't mistake your fancy for fact. Any stimulation could be fatal for you. Better that you get treatment and observe abstention."

The physician took Pandu under his care and advised him to consult the master sage for a spiritual cure.

The medicines and meditation made the desired impact. Pandu was pacified. He reconsidered the issues confronting and confounding him. The sage had lightly advised him to ascertain what he desired-whether he was still a householder or had he renounced. If he had renounced, he ought to forget about the female flesh and a son and engage in spiritual pursuits. Otherwise he could opt for the material means and resort to the prescribed 'appointee' to realise his goal.

Another sleepless might behind him, Pandu still grappled with the problem.

In the evening, when he could manage some moments of privacy, Pandu sat down beside Kunti who was engrossed in stitching her old clothes.

He talked about Hastinapur where he belonged as the rightful king; about Dhritrashtra who seemed intent upon usurping his kingdom; about their prospects of getting a son, of course, through an 'appointee.'

Pandu lingered at the last point. "There is nothing wrong in that, my lady," he said. "God has created only man and woman, and his intention is creation. You may be knowing that the man-woman relations are regulated in various ways among different societies. Even an illegitimate son was recognised by a society and several rishis still validate a child."

"I know that. How? The sage Durvasa had told me that when a woman started menstruating, it was obligatory upon her to procreate. A son was a son, even if illegitimate. As long as the woman was independent, the blood relations were determined through the mother only; and then the illegitimate son was socially as honourable as a legitimate son! Since the man had commanded sway over society, the blood relations have come to be determined through man; and the women's rights are diminishing in proportion to the increase in the value of the inheritance of property. This is all men's conspiracy."

"Well?"

"And the sage Durvasa said that if a woman was without a husband post menstruation, she should think of some deity and, perceiving a noble man as the representative of that deity, should get a divinely gifted child from him."

"That's exactly what I submit!" Pandu was thrilled with excitement.

"So you will accept an illegitimate son?"

"No, my lady!" Pandu said, "It is the sages' perception. Such sons are not recognised by the regal society any more. But they recognise a divinely gifted son brought forth by a woman, with her husband's consent, through an appointee in the absence of a legitimate son. As you are my wedded wife, a son brought forth by you will be entitled to the kingdom of Hastinapur."

Kunti was reminded of her little son. Should she divulge all to Pandu? But he had been repeatedly harping on the unacceptability of such a son.

"What do you say?" Pandu asked.

"I will consider it!" Kunti replied.

Which meant she was ready. Pandu was reassured.

63

Disregarding the charioteer's request, Bhishma had handled the reins and was now driving the vehicle at an unrestrained pace representing his state of emancipation and joy.

He had left Hastinapur far behind-not only the settlements beside the city ramparts but even their fields and barns. Now he was to himself with the pristine waters of the Ganga and the free-flowing wind. Oh, if he could be the wind or at best a bird flying spontaneously on its shoulders! That was but a wishful thinking. Truely, he was a bonded being restricted by various pledges, resolves and norms.

He halted his chariot, unbridled the horses, took them to the stream and patted them on the rumps, "You too, go and enjoy the liberty and freedom."

He sat down upon a rock and suspended his feet into the stream, which always refreshed and rejuvenated him, liberating him from all tensions.

The news of Yudhisthir's birth conveyed to him that morning thrilled him no end and in that he envisaged the advent of his redeemer. Now he could look forward to days of respite he had always longed for.

His enthusiasm was short-lived. He thought of Chitrangada, Vichitravirya, Dhritrashtra and then Pandu, and was reasonably despondent. Would this Yudhisthira deliver? Why, Dhritrashtra, Pandu, Vidur, Kunti, Madri,

Gandhari, Ambika and Ambalika were there to assist and support him. So, why Bhishma?

It was Ma Satyavati who had inhibited him.

Bhishma was fickle. Didn't he want to compel the whole universe dance to his tune? As if he would obstruct the very will of the Creator!

He pulled his feet out of the stream. Should he not retire to a far-off; secluded spot and dwell there in a hut anonymously?

The sun was withdrawing as Bhishma drove back to Hastinapur, blissful to have lived out his day in the peaceful proximity of nature.

Summoned by Satyavati, when Bhishma went to see her, he found her apparently concerned. Wasn't she happy at the birth of Pandu's son?

"Perhaps you are not aware of what has happened after that?" Satyavati complained. "Dhritrashtra's wife Gandhari is sick with symptoms of miscarriage. The bleeding won't stop. The physicians have surrendered. Should I celebrate the birth or mourn the miscarriage?"

"But it is strange. She has been receiving the best of care," Bhishma spoke in disbelief.

"That is how Providence works. Nothing is -announced beforehand. It is always a bolt out of the blue... I have called for Krishna Dvaipayana who is a skilled physician. He has arrived and is with Dhritrashtra. I believe he can do wonders," Satyavati blurted.

"Don't worry," Bhishma tried to console her.

"Why?" Satyavati's resentment was apparent. "Why, no male is born complete here. Chitrangada did not live a full life. Vichitravirya was deprived of a long life and children. Dhritrashtra is born-blind. Pandu has run away. Vidur is a maid's son. And now, catastrophe is striking before birth!"

Her dilemma was beyond Bhishma's understanding.

Vyasa was concerned too, but unlike Satyavati.

Bhishma's presence gladdened him, which was reciprocated by a warm hug from Bhishma.

"I have given the medicine. The bleeding has stopped. There is no danger of miscarriage now. The child in the womb is healthy. That way, there is no cause to worry. But ...," Vyasa told Satyavati.

"But what?

"Gandhari is suffering from a sickness even I can't cure. It's infectious and, if not contained, could devastate the whole Kuru dynasty." Vyasa elaborated. "Gandhari's bleeding was not caused by any physical factor. In fact, she was hit externally. The motive was foeticide and malice is the culprit."

"Malice is the culprit, granted. But, who did it?" Satyavati was outraged. That one deserved severe punishment.

"Gandhari herself," Vyasa announced.

"Gandhari? But, why should a woman kill her own foetus?" Satyavati was puzzled.

"Why does one commit suicide?" Vyasa posed a counter question.

"Because they are deeply in grief of which there is no remedy?" Satyavati replied.

"No!" Vyasa said, "Grief does not exist. In material conditions, there is only comfort and discomfort. Man lives through all sorts of affliction and privation. The grief is nourished by one's mental disorder. One nurtures that demon and surrenders to it."

"What has Gandhari got to do with that?" Satyavati asked.

"When Gandhari learnt about Yudhisthira's birth, the first and the only thing that occurred to her was that now her son will be junior to Yudhishthira and hence not the crown prince. Meaning thereby, she won't be the queen mother. Hence!" Vyasa explained.

Bhishma was stunned: Gandhari's aspirations were

stifled by Yudhishthira's birth. Gandhari and Dhritrashtra have still not conceded that actually the kingdom of Hastinapur was not theirs but Pandu's.

Vyasa was reasonably right that Gandhari was suffering from the 'malice' disease which was infectious. Malice would breed malice and that would end in the collapse of the Kuru clan.

Bhishma had welcomed Yudhisthira's birth as the emergence of new hopes and expectations for the Kuru. But....

64

Yudhishthira was learning to walk. Pandu had been working on him for days. When eventually Yudhisthira walked a few paces on his own, Pandu the father was full of pride and glee.

Pandu's joy knew no bounds. He wanted to share it with someone. With Kunti? No, she must be engaged in some routine task of the ashram. He decided to return to his hut, where he was joined by Madri who had watched him from her cottage.

"Madri! You know," Pandu could not restrain his excitement. "Today, Yudhisthira walked a few steps, without my support."

"That's gladdening," Madri was conspicuously formal. She had grown wary of Pandu's lately acquired philosophical bent of mind. "I see, you are very fond of children!"

"Everyone is."

"Butdon't you think this is not a fit place to rear them?"

"Why?" Pandu contended. "Climate-wise, this place is very good. The people here are very nice-righteous and generous."

"It has no splendour worthy of princes. A child brought up here could at best become an ordinary ashram-dweller, a hermit or a rustic," said Madri.

"What do you want?"

"When do we return to Hastinapur?"

"When we accomplished what we have initiated."

"But you have begotten one son!"

"I want five-seven sons. I am Pandu of the royal Kuru dynasty. I will snatch from nature the right to enjoyment."

"Any hopes?"

"I feel I am improving my masculine strength. The master physician says I will soon become a complete man. The moment my expectations are ripe for a legitimate son or I get one, the king will march to his kingdom."

"I will be the happiest then and feel I am back from hell to my life," Madri said.

"I can understand," Pandu responded and followed Yudhisthira out of the hut and came across the sage superior (Kulapati) who had meanwhile lifted Yudhisthira in his arms and blessed him.

The Kulapati left the child back on the ground. His parting words to Pandu were, "Expand the horizon of your self. Help every weak one acquire strength and be delighted in the process. You will see how joyful life is."

Back in his cottage, Pandu ruminated about the Kulapati's exhortation. That there were other children in the ashram besides his own. They claimed equal affection and care. Why Yudhisthira alone? But could he be so altruist? No! He was staying at the hermitage but was no hermit himself.

His sole dream was to beget an heir, whether legitimate or otherwise, who could occupy the throne of Hastinapur. Why, Kunti was pregnant a second time.

"Have you been out for wood-cutting?" he asked Kunti who was just back and looked tired.

"No! I'm not left with such strength! While wishing for this child, I had invoked the wind god prior to going in for the ritual cohabitation and regarded the appointed one as his representation. Seems it is a Bheema (heavy child) this time in my womb. I think this ought to be the last one from me. No more! I can't endure it anymore."

"Madri pleaded we returned to Hastinapur," Pandu digressed.

Kunti did not respond.

65

"So very handsome and healthy boy, ven'ble Queen!" the maid told Gandhari as she laid him beside her.

Gandhari was tempted to peel off the blind-fold and have a glimpse of her son. However, she managed to restrain herself and, instead, touched the baby boy carefully.

"Is he sleeping?"

"Yes Queen! The little king is asleep."

How sweet! 'The little king! Will her son be the king of Hastinapur? She was reminded of her envious outburst at the news of Kunti's son's birth and how she had attempted foeticide, for she would not see her son in any other garb.

"The king? Was he informed?"

"First of all, O Queen! He is waiting. Shall I call him?"

"Bring him in."

Dhritrashtra took the newborn in his arms and asked about his health. He insisted that the master physician should be called at one.

Gandhari could see through his mind. He was only being scrupulous. Was this newborn boy affected in any way on account of his father's blindness? And Gandhari herself had attempted the foeticide!

"Gandhari! We will name him Suyodhana for he has well (su) fought his battle (Yodhana) so far. And a tough and long battle awaits him in the future."

"Fight he surely will," Gandhari seconded him. "But it is you who have to secure him. If you don't, there won't be any battle."

"Don't you worry about that. I will definitely do that. Shakuni is no mean asset in facilitating our task."

Dhritrashtra addressed the council where he proposed: Prince Yudhisthira is senior to Prince Suyodhana and, therefore, he will be the crown-prince of Hastinapur. We have no doubts about that-you and me. But what I would like to know-will Suyodhana get the kingdom of Hastinapur after Yudhisthira?

There was a hush and then a murmur. The councillors, apparently, did not endorse Dhritrashtra's proposal.

Bhishma wanted to rebuke Dhritrashtra: Obviously, he was contriving to deprive Pandu's sons of his kingdom, wherefore Dhritrashtra was liable to condemnation. Instead of asking for Pandu's honourable return from Mount Shatshring and coronation or his son Yudhisthira's consecration as the crown-prince; he was audacious enough to demand the kingdom for his own son. Such practice did not bode well for the society. If Dhritrashtra was left unleashed, he would act like a despot.

It was Vidur's turn to rise and speak.

"Hon'ble King!" he said, "First of all, let it be decided who is the ruler. If you are the king, it must follow that Suyodhana will be the crown-prince. Then Yudhisthira stands nowhere in the picture. But, if as you concede, Yudhisthira is the crown-prince, then after him the kingdom will go to his son or, in case he has none, to his younger brother. If you propose that after Yudhisthira the kingdom should be handed over to Suyodhana, then you are putting hurdles in the path of Pandu and Yudhisthira's posterity."

"But this kingdom was mine, which was denied to me due to my blindness. Now I have a son who is sound in sight," Dhritrashtra protested.

"In fact, the kingdom was Bhishma's. My personal

submission is that Suyodhana be best kept at a safe distance from the throne. His proximity to it will only breed rivalry and antagonism within the royal dynasty, which spells doom for them," Vidur pleaded.

Dhritrashtra was fairly discontented with Vidur's plea and sought the brahmins' opinion.

"We fully endorse with Vidur, the expert one in matters of religion and ethics," the brahmins were unanimous in their verdict.

Dhritrashtra was resentful and acrimonious. He wanted to speak against the intellectuals and stop all allowances and amenities from the crown. However, then he refrained from making his intentions public and preferred reticence.

Then Dhritrashtra tried to obtain the minister's consent but they also toed Vidur's line.

Bhishma kept silent all through. His silence encouraged Dhritrashtra to turn to him for approval but his good sense argued that he was not coming forward with any remarks for he was also with the majority.

Presently the emissaries dispatched to the Shatashring mountain were back and at the court to report.

"King Pandu is hale and hearty with his family," they said. "Queen Kunti has given birth to another son who is extraordinarily big and robust. He is named Bhima."

There was much more from the messengers but Dhritrashtra was too stunned to give ear to that. So Yudhisthira had a crown-prince now-Bhima! Which meant, all the likelihood of Suyodhana getting to rule, if any, were bleak. Only due to Dhritrashtra's blindness. Oh God!

66

"Noble One!" Madri offered the master physician's medicine to Pandu. "How long have you been taking this potion since?"

"Quite long. Why?"

"Any improvement or was it just an exercise in gulping down the bitter herbs?"

Madri was bluntly outspoken but Kunti was very different and gentle.

"The Ayurvedacharya claims improvement."

"What do you think?"

"It doesn't matter what I think, only my action will prove which I am not allowed for now."

Madri mumbled something disagreeable about Pandu's libidinal state and else.

"What do you want?" Pandu was indignant.

"Already a junior queen, I was Kunti's subordinate. Now she will be the mother of three sons, and me a childless woman. I am not jealous of didi Kunti yet I do feel inferior. She is your wife and so am I, why then she alone would bring forth all your sons?"

"What do you want - pleasures of congress or of matrimony?" Pandu was straight forward.

"I want the pleasures of congress, of course, but not adultery. So, matrimony will gratify me," Madri responded.

Her words perturbed Pandu and his confidence was again at test.

He decided to consult Kunti who was with her third child, in advanced stage, for whom she had invoked the god king Indra.

He found Kunti concerned for him.

"I am worried for Yudhisthira and Bhima."

"Amidst these pristine surroundings?"

"May they be spared the step-mother's curse."

"Has Madri said something to that effect?" Kunti could smell the sinister.

"Yes," Pandu said. "What ails her is that you are on to have a third child; and she has not one. By the way, which deity you will be invoking for the fourth after Arjuna?"

"Which Arjuna?" she was puzzled.

"Our third son."

"He is still unborn and you have already named him?"

"Isn't it a good name?"

"It is," Kunti said. "But if we have a girl this time?"

"No way! Indra will not get you a girl."

"Agreed," she said. "But let me be very clear, I am not going for a fourth child from an appointed man."

"Then, listen to me. Tell Madri what Durvasa had told you by way of advice. That will save you from adultery and Madri will get a son. She will become a mother from a step-mother."

Kunti at once consented and even suggested Ashvini Kumar for 'niyoga'. "Maybe your health will also improve by their grace, and we get another handsome and healthy son."

There was no malice or ill-will in Kunti's mind against Madri.

Pandu was fairly relieved and pleased.

"Let your wish be fulfilled," he said.

67

Following the formal ceremonies pertaining to the birth and naming of the five Pandavas, the Kulpati blessed them. "Sons, always tread the path of morals and justice. God observed certain laws while creating this world and these laws are observed in its operation. These laws are the very truth. And you have to stick to them."

He sprinkled the holy water on the boys.

"What is morality?" Pandu asked him on his way to his cottage. My grandma Ganga left my grandfather Shantanu. Is it moral for a wife?"

The sage smiled, "Ganga and Shantanu's times were different. Ganga belonged to a society where a woman lives her life on her own terms. In the Uttar Kuru, the man-woman relations are still very permissive and there is no concept of the husband-wife relations in that society. The common people around this Shatshring follow polyandry and the royal clans in Aryavarta recognise polygamy. It varies with place and time. Compared to Kuru-Jangal, in Panchala, a woman is more liberated, and polyandry still prevails there. An illegitimate child is recognised by the sages but not by the regal clans. Who knows what happens in future." The sage entered his cottage, "This is a social order, O King."

In his cottage, the sage continued, "I am talking of the general morality. When we say 'speak the truth', that doesn't mean it will rain nectar from heaven. It is only

dawned on her, she gave out a loud, heart-rending cry.

The pyre was prepared as directed by the Kulapati.

"Son Yudhisthira!" he said. "Light your father's pyre."

But he was stopped by Kunti who offered to be burnt on the same pyre with her husband.

"No!" Madri screamed. "This can't be. I will share the pyre with the Noble One."

"I am senior. So this is my prerogative," Kunti pleaded.

"I am responsible for his death. Let me atone. You are senior, Didi. You are great. And generous. Let me go with the Noble One," Madri said.

Tears appeared in Kunti's eyes. She put her right hand upon Madri's head. And then she could not control herself. She burst out and cried inconsolably. She hugged Madri for a last time.

68

They collected the ashes of Pandu and Madri, made a bundle and carried it to the ashram led by the Kulapati. The last to trudge along was the eight-year old Yudhishthira, his head grimly bowed. A group of inmates made a sort of shield around him.

Inside the hermitage, the bundle was hung on a tree.

Kunti sat in the front yard of her cottage. Sahadeva, Nakul, Bhima and Arjun clung to her. Most of the women inmates flocked around.

"Kunti! What's your decision now?" The Kulapati addressed her.

"About?"

"About your future and these children's!"

A bolt from the blue!

Was Pandu her last and only link to the ashram, that death had snapped?

"Where shall I go with these little ones? I am away from my kin, physically, and emotionally too."

"Why so humble and scared? You don't have to be so desperate," the Kulpati encouraged her. "And, neither are your sons orphaned. If nowhere else, you have this ashram. But! But, King Pandu had not wished for sons so that they would spend their life doing penance in some ashram. Of course, we have many brahmin boys here. But, these are kshatriya sons. Their place is in palace. This Yudhishthira is the crown-prince of Hastinapur. Don't deprive him of his right. Honour your husband's wish who always longed for an heir."

"Everyone in this world has wishes that were unfulfilled. The king gave his life after his desire. Madri climbed the pyre with her unfulfilled desire. Now, I wish to live a pious life with my sons in this ashram," Kunti said.

"These are your sons. You may rear them the way you will. But, I will advise you not to force your conclusions on them ... Introduce them to the world. They have seen a life of penance and meditation here. Let them see the worldly life now. Then they will decide upon their kind of life."

"Their kind of life?" Kunti said. "Why, they want a life of peace and contentment. They are so happy here. And you ask us to leave this place!"

"Look at your sons here," the Kulapati said as he pointed to the five Pandavas. "They who are entitled to a royal life are living here as destitutes. They have nothing

to learn here... You have no aspirations for you are a prisoner of the happenings in your own life. But these boys have a lot to give to life. Don't obstruct the progress of your sons through your ignorance. This is sin... Also it is compulsory to take the ashes of King Pandu and Queen Madri to Hastinapur. There, their last rites will be performed with due royal grace."

"And how will I travel to Hastinapur with these five boys when we are left with no servants, chariots and horses?"

"That's no concern," the Kulapati offered. "The sages and their sons travel on foot. We will go with you up to Hastinapur, which is our duty. And if the ashes of the King and the queen are not taken to the kingdom, there will be no funeral ceremonies for the king, which will hamper the coronation of the next king. Rise, O daughter! Prepare for the journey. We will leave for Hastinapur tomorrow morning."

69

The Kulapati halted at Hastinapur's Vardhaman Gate.

The sentry was baffled. There were so many old mendicants, young recluses, a woman around thirty who looked not a forest-dweller nor a citizen. With them were five small boys.

"Inform the king that some sages have arrived," the Kulapati said. "We are here to hand over Queen Kunti, King Pandu's five divinely bestowed sons, and the ashes of King Pandu and Queen Madri."

The sentry stood dumb founded. It took the fact some time to sink in. And when it did, a bunch of horsemen were rushed to the palace.

Kunti, reasonably exhausted, sat down beneath a tree. The kids were no less tired.

She spread a sheet of cloth in the shade and laid Nakul and Sahdeva there. Arjun sat beside them. Bhima, who looked the least done-up, observed the surroundings curiously. Such a big river! The Ganga amazed him. Yudhisthira, who, as usual, looked more grave then weary, had sat aside. This mishap had cast a mantle of guardianship on him. "Are you tired, Ma?" many a time had he enquired of Kunti throughout the way and assuaged his little brothers. "Don't be cruel to them," he had admonished Bhima who would snap the leaves and flowers, roll the rocks with his feet and hit some animal or bird with a stone. "These are also living beings like you. They have life and they also feel pain."

This was Hastinapur, Kunti mused. "She was the queen of this kingdom! She recalled her grand welcome on her first arrival here. And now a widow, she sat with her sons at the gate. She knew not if she had anyone here to call her own.

A chariot with the royal ensign on it made its way out of the gate.

It left the highway and halted where they were camping.

Kunti watched. The man to descend the vehicle was Vidur.

Kunti realised Vidur had not wasted a moment upon receiving the news. He wore an ordinary long-cloth and no ornaments; sadness at his brother's demise was writ large on his whole self.

"Bhabhi!" he kneeled down at her feet.

"I am here at the royal threshold with your nephews," she choked.

The kids touched Vidur's feet in veneration. Vidur was reminded of Dhritrashtra's sons-Suyodhana and Sushasana-who had been ever reluctant to touch his feet, to show him any respect.

Next to arrive was Bhishma.

He looked slightly changed and a tad tired now. He helped Ma Satyavati get down the chariot. Satyavati looked quite old; she was not tired, but broken. She must have wept all the way and let the vital force suck out of her.

Satyavati rushed her fastest to Kunti, who pitied her.

"See what God has done to me, my daughter," Satyavati sobbed out her soul. "He would never see me happy. He takes away whosoever tends to be my support. This throne of Hastinapur is a real killer! It kills its occupants."

Satyavati hugged Kunti and cried and mourned. She would scream, cry, fight God, and beat her chest and head in turn.

Kunti forgot her own grief and endeavoured to soothe Ma Satyavati.

Bhishma came down to the Kulapati .

Next he met Kunti who broke out in tears as she touched his feet.

Bhishma put his protective hand on her to reassure her. "I am really unfortunate," he said. "I have had to witness the death of my father, of Chitrangada and Vichitravirya. And, now Pandu! I sometimes muse why God awarded me such a long life... so that I will live and endure this all. His ways are so strange. Good that you have returned to Hastinapur. No other place can provide you such comfort as your home would. I have sent a word to Dhritrashtra and Maharshi Vedvyasa, who are due here any moment now. I have talked to the Kulapati, who will march back to Shatashring with his saintly retinue after some rest. After the last rites performed on the ashes of Pandu and Madri, we will spend the twelve days of mourning here on the banks of the Ganga and then enter Hastinapur."

In the meanwhile, Dhritrashtra and Gandhari arrived there with Suyodhana and Sushasana - royally attired, Kunti observed.

Dhritrashtra lamented. He cried a few times, "My brother! If Yama (the god of death) was after a life, why? he should have killed me! Why you?"

Kunti was too numb to react.

Bhishma asked Suyodhana to embrace his brothers.

"These?" Suyodhana did not conceal his disgust.

"Why?" Bhishma said. "These are your brothers."

"So shabby!"

"Hold your tongue!" Gandhari scolded him. "They have been travelling."

Bhishma stayed away from the squabble. He called Suyodhana and Yudhisthira together and pushed them into embrace. "These are your brothers," he said. "A brother has to be loved, in whatever condition. You have to live together amicably all your life."

"Pitamaha (grandfather)! Are they here to stay?" Suyodhana said.

"Hastinapur is their home. Back from a trip or sojourn, one lives at their home," Bhishma offered.

"But where is a palace for them?" he said.

"If there is no palace, we will build one," Bhishma replied.

"Why a new one!" Gandhari blurted. "They will share our place. Two palaces are not required for a single family." And she turned to scold Suyodhana. "Now, you hold your tongue. Don't you ever interfere when the elders are talking."

Kunti was vexed: Why no one was talking, or referring to it as the homecoming of the master of Hastinapur. No one said he would reside in King Pandu's palace, occupy his throne. She felt like, caught in a crisis, they had come to take shelter like their dependents. A lot had changed at Hastinapur. The caretakers had not only grabbed their place but even forgot about the real master.

Dhritrashtra looked conspicuously worried. What ailed him Bhishma wondered-Pandu's demise or Kunti and the Pandavas' return?

70

On the thirteenth day of mourning, the royal family and the eminent citizens entered the town.

Vedvyasa approached Ma Satyavati to beg her leave.

"Why all this, my son?" Satyavati shed tears, her voice choked. "Why is it with me alone that the plank on which I pin my hopes vanishes into the blue?"

"Not hopes, Ma! Say desires," Vyasa said.

"Desires all right! What's wrong with the desires? Is desire a sin?"

"No, Ma. Both desire and peace are not to be wished at once. Desire is an amalgamation of weal and woe : instead of, it represents unrest. If you want not woe, don't want weal."

"As a mother, I witnessed the death of my sons and grandson. What else is there in store for me? God would better summon me," Satyavati lamented.

"Ma!" Vyasa stepped forward to solace Satyavati. "You are suffering as you are bound by your previous wishes and now you make another wish. This is a bonded stage and a bonded being is never happy. Liberate yourself from these bonds. This is not your stage to be bonded but to strive for emancipation."

"Do you never have a desire? Are you never unhappy? Are you absolutely liberated? If that's so, I will forsake God and take refuge in you."

"Don't seek refuge in me, Ma! Come to my ashram. Come out of these mundane surroundings. Come, live with me. Observe my way of life, you must now renounce the material world."

"Without making arrangements for the Kuru clan? You think I am going to die. Let me tell you, nothing is happening to me." Satyavati said.

Vyasa was amazed at his mother's stubborn lust for worldly affairs. "When Time summons, there is no leave for making arrangements. It is to be accomplished by those who are left behind," Vyasa was soft but stern. "Come to my ashram, I am also your son."

"And Hastinapur?"

"Bhishma is there."

"Bhishma is very shrewd. He knows the throne of Hastinapur is murderous. Therefore, he would not occupy it himself. He enthrones one who he considers his enemy and that one is consumed by death," Satyavati spoke insanely.

"Dvaipayana desires to take me with him," Satyavati said to Bhishma who had just stepped in.

"Ma! A son can ask his mother to come along but not move away from him," Vyasa answered for Bhishma.

"You have long maintained silence, Bhishma!" Satyavati said. "You have suppressed yourself greatly, my son! And I have been the greatest cause behind that."

Vyasa was astonished. Ma Satyavati had just called Bhishma shrewd.

Satyavati further said to Bhishma : instead of, "My son! This day I do release you from your bond. I absolve you from both your pledges. I am going to Dvaipayana's ashram with him. I wish Ambika and Ambalika to accompany me. I leave you behind. You may take charge of the kingdom until Yudhisthira comes of age."

Vyasa laughed : instead of, "Are you releasing Bhishma, Ma, or once again putting him in bond?"

His mother was a virtual riddle to Vyasa: Had her sublimity risen its head now and she was releasing Bhishma out of compunction? Or, had she really come to believe in the so-called murderousness of Hastinapur's throne and wanted to have Bhishma killed by making him sit upon that.

"I will take care of Pandu and Dhritrashtra's children, Ma!" Bhishma assured Satyavati.

"Happy."

Bhishma stood still.

Ambika readily prepared to leave with Satyavati. She wished to see Vidur before leaving.

"Vidur?" Satyavati asked.

"Yes, ma!"

"Not Dhritrashtra and Gandhari?"

"No!"

"Go! See them!"

Ambika blessed Vidur and said, "I am leaving with Ma Satyavati to dwell in the forest. I am highly obliged to your mother who had saved me in hard times. Now I beg you: Protect my child in my absence."

Vidur reassured her.

"Don't you ever support him unfairly. Howsoever he may protest, never shall you let him deviate from morality. Even if he considered you his enemy, don't you ever support what is unfair."

"I promise."

Bhishma met Vyasa very late in the night and raised questions about her being taken away against her will. Vyasa convinced him it was in her interest, for her well-being.

"Will she get peace there?" Bhishma asked.

"I will try."

"Any chances of her return?"

"A sick person should not return to the causes of sickness."

"You know better!" Bhishma said and left.

Next morning, the entire royal family was assembled at the main gate of Hastinapur. The horsemen and chariots were a part of the retinue which had Bhishma in the lead, accompanied by Vyasa and Queen Mother Satyavati in the same chariot.

Bhishma was the first to step down. He was followed

by Vyasa who helped Ma Satyavati get down the vehicle.

From the chariots got down Ambika, Ambalika, Dhritrashtra, Gandhari, Kunti, Suyodhana, Sushasana and Bhima.

The people thronging the gate were numerous but conspicuously silent. They apprehended something sinister coming their way.

Vyasa embraced Bhishma, blessed Dhritrashtra, Gandhari, Kunti and the kids, and said : instead of, "May you all be happy. Now you may return. We will walk the remaining length as it is not advisable to ride a chariot on exile." And turning to Satyavati, he said, "Come, Ma!'

Satyavati was obviously reluctant. She stepped back, kissed Dhritrashtra, Gandhari and Kunti, and hugged the children. "I will be back soon," she said.

Virtually, Satyavati dragged herself. She was leaving Hastinapur but was Hastinapur leaving her?

Satyavati paused before Bhishma, looked at him, tears swelling in her eyes, and she lowered her head and said, "Take care of the Kuru clan."

As Bhishma watched her being led away, his heart was wrenched for himself.

He wished he would confront Vyasa and question him: "Why don't you seize my arm that way and steer me too out of Hastinapur?"

But he had to retrace his steps: Before him were sightless Dhritrashtra, blindfolded Gandhari, and an apprehensive Kunti with her children.

He stood flanked by Yudhisthira and Suyodhana, his hands rested respectively on their shoulders. He eyed the receding figures of Satyavati, Ambika and Ambalika longingly, as a traveler about to start his journey watches one who, his journey completed, has reached his destination or as a prisoner watches his mate going out of jail towards freedom.

□□